THE PERSIAN CAPER

BY BILL BURKE

BeachHouse Books, Chesterfield Missouri USA

Copyright

ISBN 9781596300699

Library of Congress Cataloguing in Publication Data

Library of Congress Cataloging-in-Publication Data

Burke, Bill, 1935-

The Persian Caper / by Bill Burke.

p. cm.

ISBN 978-1-59630-069-9 (alk. paper)

1. Iran--Fiction. 2. International relations--Fiction. 3. Nuclear warfare--Prevention--Fiction. I. Title.

PS3602.U75516P47 2011

813'.6--dc22

2011019679

BeachHouse
Books

www.beachhousebooks.com

BeachHouse Books

An Imprint of
Science & Humanities Press,
Chesterfield, Missouri, USA

DEDICATION

I dedicate this book to my Persian, Armenian, and American business colleagues, friends, and casual acquaintances whom I associated with during my assignment in Iran. I also dedicate it to my lovely wife, Anita, who was my constant companion during our travels throughout the Middle East, Near East, and North Africa.

ACKNOWLEDGEMENTS

To my wife, Anita, and the associates in my writers' group, I thank all of you for your encouragement, support, and invaluable critiques while I developed the manuscript for this tale.

Additionally, I acknowledge my good friend, Leo, for his review of my first manuscript draft. Leo's military intelligence background, and his liaison experience with domestic and foreign intelligence agencies, were extremely useful during his review and certainly added credibility to my novel.

A final thank you goes to another good friend, Rich, for his review of my final manuscript draft. He is an avid reader of spy novels, and his suggestions proved to be very helpful during this polishing phase of my manuscript development.

PREFACE

This story is a work of fiction and does not depict actual events, except for factual historical incidents, including recent headline news. An experienced writer and colleague of mine, Maris, acknowledged my work with the following comment, "I think we all agree that Bill's spy novel is exciting, contemporary, and relevant to what's going on in today's world." I certainly hope that she is correct. This is an action-packed story of five secret agents and the intrigue, danger, and suspense involved in their exciting espionage vocations. My tale is laced with real, state-of-the-art surveillance equipment (Micro Aerial Vehicles), weapons (Massive Ordinance Penetrators), aircraft (Miniature Air-Launched Decoys), and satellite communications systems (Advanced Extremely High Frequency).

All of my characters are fictitious, and any names of actual people used for my characters, living or dead, are purely coincidental. Indeed, I selected many of the given and surnames at random from ethnic name lists available on the Internet. Nevertheless, the characters are realistic, with all-to-human foibles and emotions. An occasional touch of irony enhances the character descriptions.

I visited many of the locations mentioned in my story and became familiar with the local customs, various ethnic cuisines, and peoples while traveling throughout the Middle East, Near East, and North Africa. Morocco, Egypt, Jordan, Israel, Syria, Turkey, and Iran are some of the countries I visited in that vast, volatile region of the globe.

As an American expatriate, I was entranced with mysterious, alluring Persia! Shah Reza Khan changed the nation's name to Iran during 1935. However, the locals still called it Persia in their everyday conversations when I was there, and I believe many of them also call it Persia today. I lived, worked, and studied in Tehran, Iran for a year during

1978. While employed in my consulting position, I visited a number of locations in the nation, including Ahvaz, Bandar-e-Abbas, Isfahan, Kerman, Tabriz, and Yazd.

I visited many more locations in Iran with my wife during our free time. During these excursions, we thoroughly enjoyed the people, food, and sights at Chalus, Hamadan, Karaj, Parchin, Persepolis, Qom, Rey, Shemshak, Shiraz, and a dozen other small villages and towns. Our Persian travels also took us to the huge Dasht-e-Kavir and Dasht-e-Lut wilderness regions, Mount Damavand and Mount Tochal in the Alborz mountain range, and tiny villages on the Caspian Sea shoreline. Many of these locations are mentioned in my story. Some of my personal observations are also included in the tale, as well as several incidents that actually happened during the time I lived there. In addition, I attended the University of Tehran, where I studied *Islamic Philosophy and Mysticism* and *Archeology of Iran*.

Some foreign words and phrases appear in my book. This was done to give the reader an impression of the countries and the local populaces in my story. Of course, the Near Eastern and Middle Eastern words are essentially spelled phonetically. The reader may refer to the Glossary for definitions of foreign terms and acronyms used in the tale.

The main protagonists, which are the heroes and heroines of the story, as well as the antagonists, may be found in the Principal Characters section. There is also a page for Location Code Names, and a Mission Timeline for quick reference of where the main characters are on any given day. The maps are my hand-drawn artist's conceptions and are certainly not to scale, with approximate locations to provide a general idea of where my tale takes place.

Please be assured, I am not advocating attacks on Iran's nuclear sites. Remember, this is a work of fiction! So, please just sit back, relax, and enjoy this exciting, yet true-to-life novel about a capricious escapade.

QUOTE

Evil unchecked grows, evil tolerated poisons the whole system.

Jawaharial Nehru

CONTENTS

THE

PERSIAN

CAPER

CHAPTER ONE: ISTANBUL

A chilly fog rolled down the Bosporus strait from the Black Sea as the sun disappeared into the Sea of Marmara and the Dardanelles strait. Patrick O'Leary, code name *Viper Leader*, zipped up his windbreaker just part way and pulled up his collar as the cold fog hit him on the back of the neck. Pat had learned during his twenty years as a CIA covert field operative to have his weapon accessible and ready for use at all times. Tonight was no exception. His Walther PPK was easy to reach in the shoulder holster and ready for combat with a round in the chamber.

While walking toward Galata Tower from the Princes Islands ferry slip in a relaxed alertness state, Pat suddenly sensed he was being watched. This feeling was not unusual. He was young looking for being in his late-forties. In addition, his Adonis-like features, trim six-foot stature, curly black hair, sexy hazel eyes, and slightly dark Mexican-Irish complexion always seemed to attract members of the opposite sex. However, the feeling was different this time and he thought, *Danger lurks! Be alert.*

He removed his Polaroid sunglasses as dusk settled over Istanbul, and then glanced at the mirror-like lens as he put them in a case. The image confirmed his suspicion when he saw a furtive figure peeking around a building about a block behind him. Pat mused, *Aha, the same fellow that eyed me on the ferry! Now I'm sure he's a SVR agent.* The SVR, an official successor of the KGB, is Russia's primary external intelligence agency, and their agents were always spying on Pat to see what he was doing. Nonetheless, aware of a specific threat, and in a red alert state now, Pat's right hand has a firm grip on the Walther and he is ready for anything that might happen.

1

An *imam's* captivating call to prayer emitted from a mosque minaret in the direction of the Golden Horn inlet in the center of enchanting Istanbul. Pat entered the bright-blue Iznik tiled Tunel Metro station to catch the Galata Hill subway train. Then his BlackBerry vibrated and a text message read, *"viper leader. andrei desnov, svr, following you. will delay him. cobra."* He felt a warm glow, knowing that his Mossad colleague, *Cobra,* had his back covered.

The CIA had not sanctioned a hit on Desnov, so Pat responded with, *"cobra. as i suspected. don't harm him, divert him. he's just curious. viper leader."*

Andrei Desnov is a stocky, muscular White Russian with a scarred rock-like face, white hair, and steel-gray eyes. A citizen of the Russian Federation now, he was a Soviet KGB agent in Afghanistan during the 1980s while the Russians were fighting the Taliban. He was transferred into the Foreign Intelligence Service (SVR) when Russia's President Boris Yeltsin disbanded the KGB at the end of the Cold War. Desnov's long history in both agencies included involvement with training Iraqi spies during the Saddam Hussein regime, and managing multiple covert political assassinations abroad. He received top-secret information from an American spy during the 1980s and 1990s. He also received highly classified documents from another American spy during the 1990s, which led to the execution of several CIA agents in Russia.

A well-educated atheist, Desnov studied at the Moscow Institute of Economics, Management, and Law. He then earned a Bachelor of Science degree at Moscow State University. He speaks English, French, Pashtu, and Persian fluently. Married for a short while and then divorced, he is now single. Andrei translates to *Warrior*, and the word circulating throughout the CIA was, "The spy apparently tries to live up to his name."

Cobra is the code name for Zivah Benjamin, an Israeli Institute for Intelligence and Special Operations (Mossad) operative. The Hebrew name Zivah means *Splendor* in English, and the diminutive, black-haired, olive-complexioned beauty with seductive dark brown eyes is certainly a splendid specimen of Middle Eastern womanhood. She went to work for Shin Bet, the Israeli Internal Intelligence Agency, after her tour of duty in the Israeli Defense Force. Then she eventually transferred to Mossad. This highly regarded agency is responsible for Israel's covert operations and counter-terrorism activities.

Zivah caught up with Desnov, fluttered her attractive eyelashes, and smiled as she touched his arm and asked him, "Sir, can you give me directions to the Kulesi Restaurant?" *Cobra*, as petite as she was, could have quickly and easily taken out the experienced Russian agent.

The egocentric Russian took the bait and lost track of Pat while telling Zivah, "*Da*. That restaurant is located right here at the top of Galata Tower, young lady." Desnov just could not take his eyes off the beautiful, well-formed woman with exquisite silver earrings standing so close to him. Of course, he asked, "May I buy your dinner?"

Zivah looked into his steel-gray eyes and thought, *He looks like a wolf eying his prey*. Then she smiled and politely

3

replied, "No thank you, comrade," and hustled into the tower lobby.

The SVR operative shook his head in disbelief because he was rebuffed, and said, "*Daas vee daan ya!*" Desnov then headed toward the Tunel station to locate Pat.

Zivah understood his curt Russian goodbye. She could have assassinated Desnov, with the poison-tipped needle hidden in her silver ring when she touched his arm. However, she followed Pat's orders and did not give him a fatal injection.

Pat got off the train at the top of Galata Hill near Tunel Square. The tempting aromas of Turkish coffee, *baklava*, roasted chestnuts, and exotic cuisine mingled and tickled his nose as he walked along Istikal Caddesi. Melodic Near Eastern music wafted from open windows while he strolled through the shopping district along with tourists and local families. He mused, *This is the heart and soul of Istanbul. I love this city!*

After making sure that Desnov was no longer following him, Pat stepped into an unmarked doorway. The overwhelming aroma of Turkish food, and the anticipation of a fine meal, immediately hit him as he climbed three flights up a steep, dimly lit stairwell. *I sure am hungry*, he thought as his palate craved the exotic cuisine. The rooftop Hagibaba Restaurant was crowded, but the charming hostess remembered the handsome American. With a seductive smile, a flip of her auburn hair, and a twinkle in her jade-green eyes, she remarked "Nice to see you again, *efendi*," and sat him at a choice table.

Pat responded with a wide grin and a friendly, "Great to be back to enjoy your exceptional fare and your pleasing demeanor, Melike," as he reflected, *You certainly display the attributes of your Beautiful name.*

4

The Hagibaba is a gathering place for the locals, where tourists are seldom seen, and it is Pat's favorite Istanbul eating-place because all of the authentic, aromatic smorgasbord dishes are very tasty, with just hints of subtle spices. He savored the sautéed eggplant, beef and rice stuffed cabbage, long green hot peppers, and various *dolmas*, especially the grape leaves stuffed with flavorsome rice and lamb. A glass of local Kulup red wine topped off the fine meal on his last night in Turkey. This would also be his last glass of wine until he returned from Iran, a nation where alcoholic beverages are strictly forbidden.

Pat's nighttime view of the strait from the rooftop was spectacular as he observed the orange-hued Bosporus Bridge lit up like the Golden Gate Bridge near his hometown. Several tramp steamers cruised by with their running lights aglow, and multi-million-dollar luxury yachts with dazzling lights plied the busy waterway. *I'm going to miss this place*, he reflected.

On the way out, Melike whispered, "I am off in an hour."

Pat whispered back, "Maybe the next time I'm in Istanbul."

"I will pray to Allah that you will return soon."

Pat checked into the Hotel InterContinental on Taksim Square a few blocks away. Pleasant thoughts of spending time with Zivah the past few evenings lulled the secret agent into a deep, peaceful sleep.

Pat had just returned from the island of Buyukada in the Republic of Turkey, the largest of the nine Princes Islands in the Sea of Marmara. To prevent a possible unilateral attack on Iran by Israel, the CIA had arranged for a secret conference at the Splendide Hotel with a unique coalition team of CIA, OHD, Mossad, and MI6 operatives attending. The team members were handpicked by their agencies, and then approved by Pat. This elite group of five operatives: Patrick O'Leary, Alev Barak, Ari Jacobi, Logan Johnson, and Zivah Benjamin, will develop a plan to infiltrate Iran, locate and observe nuclear research and development sites within the hard-core Islamic nation, and transmit their findings to CIA headquarters at Langley, Virginia. The coalition's headquarters staffs will then decide how to coordinate military strikes on the sites.

Pat prefaced the meeting with, "After Iran's President stated publicly, 'Today the Iranian nation is standing on the nuclear height,' our allied agencies feared that Iran's leaders are preparing to develop and use nuclear weapons in an all-out *Jihad*, or Holy War, against the West. Iran's Vice President subsequently announced that the Islamic Republic has 5,000 centrifuges operating and enriching uranium, in defiance of the United Nations demand to halt the nation's nuclear program.

"American experts believe Iran now has enough fissile material to build a nuclear warhead. Moreover, the United Nations watchdog group, the International Atomic Energy Agency (IAEA), determined that Iran has already amassed more than a ton of enriched uranium. The final straw was Iran's launch of a telecommunications satellite into orbit with a Safir-2 rocket. Israel and the West believe the Safir-2 technology will also be used to propel a long-range ballistic missile, armed with a nuclear warhead, toward Israel."

Ari and Zivah nodded in agreement.

Pat continued, "Our intelligence community suspects a Holy War will include attacks on neighboring countries friendly to the West, including Turkey and especially Israel. Iran's leaders promised, with fiery rhetoric, to 'wipe Israel off the map' several times. Therefore, Israeli jets fly over Chalus, Tehran, Arak, Natanz, Isfahan, Darkhovin, Ardakan, Bushehr, and Fasa frequently to check the development progress at those sites. A nuclear-armed Iran could also spark an arms race in the Middle East. That likelihood would certainly put Israel in even more jeopardy from the Arab countries.

"Additionally, Iran is developing new uranium enrichment plants in defiance of the United Nations order to cease such development. And, the IAEA recently criticized Iran for building a secret nuclear plant in the mountains near the ancient holy city of Qom. This unfinished, underground facility will eventually contain centrifuges capable of enriching uranium at a much higher speed and efficiency than Iran's existing plants. Our team will provide the confirmation that the facilities need to be taken out."

Patrick O'Leary, a highly qualified and skilled covert agent endowed with charming charisma, was selected to lead the team of espionage agents by an agreement between the coalition's agency chiefs. He represents the American Central Intelligence Agency (CIA). The code name for the clandestine operation is "The Persian Caper."

The diverse agent speaks and reads Persian, Arabic, Spanish, and French fluently. Brilliant and scholarly, Pat had earned Bachelor of Science and Master of Science degrees at Stanford University. He also completed night classes at the University of Tehran and course work at the University of Michigan. He is a devout Catholic, and he is single but married to his job. Pat just could not find time to get really serious with members of the opposite sex. Although, he did find time for big game hunting expeditions and competitive target shooting events between assignments.

Pat was more than pleased with this assignment because he had a score to settle with the Iranians. As a young Marine Lance Corporal, he was on duty at the main entrance of the American Embassy on Takht-e-Jamsid Street in Tehran when Ayatollah Ruhollah Khomeini's Islamic militants stormed the gate and seized the compound on November 4, 1979. His Winchester Model 12, twelve-gauge pump shotgun, and his Colt Model 1911, .45-caliber semi-automatic pistol, were fully loaded. However, his unit was under strict orders from the U.S. Ambassador: "Do not shoot!" Patrick became one of the 52 hostages held captive by the militants until their release on January 20, 1981, the day President Ronald Reagan was inaugurated.

He also lost several good buddies when a Hezbollah Islamic Jihad suicide bomber drove a truck loaded with six tons of high explosives into the U.S. Marine Corps barracks in Beirut, Lebanon during October 1983. The blast leveled the huge building and killed 241 American servicemen. Islamic Jihad is part of the Shiite Hezbollah paramilitary organization in Lebanon, and the Islamic Republic of Iran supports it. Therefore, the Persian Caper would be payback time for him, and he very much relished getting the assignment!

Pat is a certified Four Weapons Combat Master, which includes expertise with handguns, shotguns, rifles, and submachine guns. Plus, he is an expert in the martial arts, and holds a Master of Close Combat title. His weapon of choice is a relatively small Walther PPK. It weighs a mere 22.4 ounces, and the 6.1 inch length, 4.3 inch height, and 1 inch width is certainly ideal for concealed carry. The .380-caliber, also called a 9x17-millimeter Short in Europe, with its 800.5 feet per second muzzle velocity is considered marginal as a man-stopper. However, Pat's exceptional shooting skills more than compensates for the lack of stopping power of the .380. He most certainly appreciates the high quality, inherent accuracy, and fine workmanship of the weapon.

Using a Crimson Trace Lasergrip sight, Pat consistently puts seven rounds in one hole at a distance of seven meters during monthly live-fire practice sessions with the Walther on the pistol range. This is a typical covert operation shooting distance. Pat prefers a shoulder holster for the weapon, however, he uses a strong side, high-rise hip holster, covered with a loose-fitting, untucked shirt while in hot climates where wearing a coat or jacket would be uncomfortable.

Alev Barak, code name *Copperhead*, represents the Turkish Special Warfare Department (OHD). Alev translates to *Flame*, and she appeared to be burning hot with desire while eyeing Pat. Smiling, with her pearl-like teeth sparkling, she greeted him with a demure, "*Selam*, Patrick!" Her earthy, curvaceous, five-foot six-inch tall body exuded sex appeal, and Pat is most certainly interested in her.

She is whimsical, voluptuous, and extremely attractive. She also knows it and is a little vain. Her distinctive Near Eastern complexion, jet-black hair, exotic coal-black eyes, and indigenous attire makes it very easy for her to blend in with any of the region's varied ethnic groups. Alev's multiple gold bracelets, dangling gold earrings, and Turkish bead necklace fit her regional profile exactly. In her late thirties, Alev could also have passed as a well-stacked belly dancer. In fact, Pat thought she resembled the sensual belly dancer he watched perform at the Kervansaray Nightclub in the Istanbul city center the previous week.

Alev is fluent in Arabic, Armenian, and English, speaks conversational Persian, and knows some Italian and French. A Sunni Muslim, she was educated at Istanbul University, but didn't receive a degree. Alev had never married and did not want to be. She is having too much fun to consider getting serious with anyone. Moreover, she is accustomed to getting her own way, especially with men.

Alev is also a top operative and well versed in the use of martial arts, knives, and firearms. She holds an expert rating with UZI submachine guns. Her personal sidearm is a Turkish-made Zigana M-16, 9-millimeter, double-action semi-auto pistol. She prefers a high-rise, cross-draw hip holster for the large weapon because it is then easier for her to reach under the folds of her loose fitting Turkish clothing.

Ari Jacobi, code name *Asp*, represents the Israeli Mossad. Ari translates to *Lion*, and he certainly is a brave, lion-hearted field agent, as proven during covert assignments in Lebanon, Syria, and Bosnia. He is in his thirties, a slim five-foot nine-inch tall handsome man, with brown eyes, dark brownish hair, and a smooth olive complexion. He also is single and never married. Pat wondered why Ari and Zivah were not involved with each other. He contemplated, *They certainly would make a nice-looking couple. Perhaps they aren't compatible, or maybe he's gay.* Ari's specialty field is nuclear weapons, including dirty bombs and missile warheads.

He speaks Persian, Arabic, French, English, and German fluently, and knows some Kurdish and Russian. A devout Jew, Ari follows Orthodox Judaism. He earned a Bachelor of Science degree at the Hebrew University of Jerusalem, and is currently working on his Master's degree.

His cousin's entire family was killed when an Iranian-made Hamas rocket, fired from the Gaza Strip, hit their home in Sderot during 2008. Therefore, he also had a score to settle with Iran.

This agent can handle himself very well in a firefight, and he is an expert with all hand-held weapons. Ari carries a SIG 228, 9-millimeter, double-action semi-auto pistol in a shoulder holster. The Mossad operative can hit the center of mass in a silhouette target at 100 meters with the very accurate and reliable sidearm. This highly developed skill is a rarity, even in the world of covert operations.

Logan Johnson, code name *Adder*, represents the British Secret Intelligence Service, MI6. His plain, non-descript, milk-toast-like looks, graying hair, shamrock-green eyes, five-foot eight-inch frame, and apparent easy-going demeanor are misleading, as he was an excellent James Bond-style spy in his younger years. He attained "Double-O" status and the license to kill early in his career and was knighted by the Queen for his brave exploits.

Logan's East London accent adds to his mystique. He was married and divorced twice, and subsequently decided to remain a bachelor the rest of his life.

While on a mission in Iran during 1982, Logan was involved in the defection of KGB officer Vladimir Kuzichkin in Tehran. He also had covert operations experience in the USSR during the 1980s. Logan was active in seeking weapons of mass destruction in Iraq during the 1990s, where he had to assassinate members of Saddam Hussein's Iraqi Intelligence Service, Mukhabarat. Prior to joining MI6, he served in the British Security Service, MI5, where he worked in the counter-terrorism unit.

Logan is fluent in Persian, Arabic, French, and Russian, and knows some Italian. A casual Episcopalian, he was educated at the University of London, where he earned a Bachelor of Science degree. Although now in his late-fifties, he can handle himself extremely well in a firefight and is an excellent covert operative.

His personal sidearm is a Beretta Px4 Storm, sub-compact, 9-millimeter, double-action semi-auto pistol, and he prefers a shoulder holster for the weapon. Logan has an Expert rating on the pistol range.

Zivah is also one of the attendees at the conference, and the sensual forty-year-old was immediately attracted to Pat. The five-foot four-inch tall woman did not waste time letting Pat know she was interested in him, and more than just professionally. Her sexy *"Shalom, Patrick!"* and her big smile gave away her intentions toward Pat. The feeling was mutual as he was smitten by the attractive young single woman and her absolutely perfect hourglass figure. Although she had dated many men, Zivah never married and had not found time to get serious enough with anyone to consider marriage. She realizes she is an attractive woman, but does not display signs of vanity.

Zivah speaks fluent Persian, Arabic, French, and English, and has some knowledge of Russian, Turkish, and Spanish. The very intelligent Jewish woman practices Reform Judaism. She earned a Bachelor of Arts degree at the Hebrew University of Jerusalem. Well trained in the martial arts, Zivah can certainly handle herself when up against opponents twice her size and weight. She had proven herself during undercover assignments in the Palestinian territories when she infiltrated Hamas, as well as during other covert assignments in Iran, Tunis, Syria, and Lebanon.

Her carry gun is a SIG 239, 9-millimeter, double-action semi-auto pistol. She prefers a strong side, high-rise hip holster, and she has a speedy draw and presentation with it. Pat believes she might even be able to out-shoot him on the range. She is also qualified as a sharpshooter with rifles, and holds expert ratings with submachine guns and pistols. While in Shin Bet, she taught agents how to effectively shoot UZI submachine guns. Moreover, she is a real pro with knives and can throw them as accurately as any circus knife performer.

Zivah also has a score to settle with the Iranians. Ali Ashtary, one of her long-time acquaintances in Tel Aviv, was executed by Iran in 2008. He was convicted and hung for being a Mossad agent and spying for Israel while he was conducting legitimate business in Tehran. Like Pat, the Persian Caper would be payback time for her.

Pat continued the meeting with the declaration, "If Iran builds and uses nuclear bombs, they will unleash an Armageddon in the Middle East. There will be warfare between Persians and Israelis; Arabs and Persians; Persians and Turks; Arabs and Israelis; Arabs and Arabs; and so forth. The now deceased Ayatollah Ruhollah Khomeini once wrote that a Holy War entails conquering *all* non-Moslem territories. Moreover, the Iran regime aids and supports the Hezbollah, Hamas, and Islamic Jihad terrorist groups. It's also important to remember that the parliament of the current *mullah*-controlled Iranian theocracy recently chanted 'Death to Israel!' and 'Death to America!' in their chambers."

Ari added, "Of course, the Iranians love to rattle their sabers!"

"Yes, they certainly do. Our mission is to provide Intel that will allow our respective nations to prevent that from happening by putting a stop to their nuclear research and development. We will enter Iran clandestinely. Then, with the help of local contacts, we will observe and verify nuclear research and development sites and transmit our findings directly to CIA Headquarters at Langley, Virginia. Our local contacts will be paid well for their dangerous assignments … $5,000 U.S. apiece."

"That's a lot of money for this region!" Alev proffered.

"It is. However, they will most certainly earn it. Continuing on, multi-agency intelligence reports indicate confirmation is needed for target locations at Chalus, Tehran, Arak, Natanz, and Isfahan. According to a *Middle East Intelligence Bulletin*, a mountain near Chalus on the Caspian Sea houses a nuclear weapons development facility. A known research reactor is located in the Tehran Nuclear Research Center in the Amir Abad district of the capital city. Near Arak is the location of a heavy-water nuclear reactor. A uranium enrichment center is located just outside of the desert town of Natanz. Finally, the Isfahan Administration Offices house the leading nuclear scientists in Iran, and the nearby Isfahan Nuclear Technology and Research Center contains the primary Iranian nuclear research and weapons program facility. I might add that we also have a mole inside the administrative offices at the university."

"If we have an opportunity to take out our assigned locations while in-country, should we?" Logan inquired.

"That's an emphatic no!" Pat then explained, "Remember, this will be just a surveillance and Intel gathering mission for us. The team will verify the nuclear sites and determine if each location is a soft or hardened target. If our agencies decide to destroy the sites, our

14

respective military forces will utilize missiles and conventional bombs on the soft targets. They will use newly developed bunker-buster bombs on the hardened underground targets, and perhaps commando raids to ensure their complete destruction. Those decisions are above my pay grade.

"Of course, there are other known nuclear research and development sites, such as the light-water nuclear reactor at Bushehr, where plutonium in the spent fuel can be used to make atomic weapons. As well as the uranium ore purification plant at Ardakan, the uranium enrichment site at Darkhovin, and the uranium conversion facility at Fasa. There is also a new facility being developed in a mountain near Qom, but it is premature to attempt to observe and verify that site as a target. However, the five selected targets are deemed the most important for our immediate observation and verification.

"I will take the Tehran target because I lived and worked there and I'm thoroughly familiar with the city and its environs. I'll also check out nearby Parchin in the desert, if I have the time. Intelligence reports indicate high-intensity explosives used to encircle enriched plutonium and uranium in nuclear implosion bombs, are being tested at that location. My local contact will be an anti-government dissident whom I befriended before the revolution."

Alev remarked, "I would like to volunteer for the Chalus target, as many of the locals in the region speak Turkish, and I have traveled to the Caspian Sea in the past. In addition, I have cousins living in Tabriz, which is en route to Chalus, and they can help me get back to Turkey after the mission, if necessary. However, I will need help with finding a local contact."

Pat replied, "We'll take care of it, Alev. That site is yours."

Ari said, "The Arak target is my choice because I have distant Jewish relatives living in nearby Hamadan that are descendants of Esther, the Jewish wife of Xerxes, and her uncle Mordecai from the Old Testament days. I'm positive I can rely on their assistance with the mission, and I'll use my great-uncle's home as a base. I also will need assistance with finding a local contact."

"You've got it, Ari. We'll take care of the contact arrangements," Pat replied.

Logan chimed in, "I opt for Natanz, Gov, because I became familiar with that area while on a top-secret covert mission in nearby Qom during the Iran-Iraq War in the 1980s." He did not discuss the details of that assignment and the other agents did not question him about it. He continued, "I also need a local contact, because it has been years since I was in-country."

Pat nodded and stated, "Will do, Logan. Natanz is your target."

Finally, Zivah remarked with a big smile, "Great! I spent some time in Isfahan during a previous covert assignment, and I would have picked that choice location anyway. Moreover, I met a young Isfahani woman during my mission, and she had expressed anti-Islamic regime leanings. She will most likely be my local contact."

"Good, Zivah. Let me know if you need help communicating with her," Pat responded.

Pat contacted CIA headquarters to provide the mission assignments and ask for assistance with finding local contacts for Alev, Ari, and Logan. Langley responded with contact names and complete dossier information within 30 minutes. All of the local contacts, and their immediate family members, were cleared for the secret mission.

Handing out the dossiers, Pat explained, "You're all good to go. HQ will notify your selected local contacts."

Pat then continued his presentation, "Alev and I will be inserted into Iran by land. We will fly to Lake Van in eastern Anatolia, then drive across the border at Kapikoy in an Iranian-made Samand, the new version of the old Paykan. Posing as husband and wife, we will drive through the Zagros Mountains to Tabriz, and then over the Talish Mountains to Chalus on the Caspian Sea."

Of course, Zivah did not care much for that part of the plan, and her eyes and body language showed her displeasure. She looked at Alev, and visualized sending her a telepathic message, *Stay away from him, Alev, or I'll scratch your eyes out.*

Pat continued, "I will meet my Iranian contact, Hossein, in Chalus. The two of us will continue on to Tehran in an Iranian-made Mercedes-Benz. Hossein translates to *Good*, and I know he will be really good at his assigned task because we had met as young adults in Tehran during 1978 and became close friends. Meanwhile, Alev will also meet her female Iranian contact, Hamideh, in Chalus. Hamideh translates to *Praiseworthy*, and her dossier indicates that she will certainly live up to her name.

"Ari will enter Iran by land. After flying to Lake Van with Alev and me, he will meet his Kurdish contact, Sadar, which means *Leader*. Ari and Sadar will drive a Land Rover into northern Iraq at Begor. Just east of Halabaja, they will cross the border into Iran via a secret pass in the Zagros Mountains in an area that is not closely observed by the Iranian Border Patrol. The two of them will then take back roads to Hamadan."

"Sounds good to me," Ari offered.

"Logan will be inserted by sea. After flying to Kuwait, via Amman, he will meet his Iranian contact, Farhad, at the airport. Logan and Farhad will take an Arab fishing *dhow* across the northern Persian Gulf waters, then up the Shatt-al-Arab waterway to Khorramshahr, Iran. From there, they will sail upstream to Ahvaz on the Karun River. The two of them will drive from Ahvaz to Ardestan, just south of Natanz, in an old Mercedes. This roundabout route is designed to avoid extremely high security at the Iranian ports on the gulf."

"An astoundingly good plan, Gov!" Logan stated.

"Zivah will enter Iran by air. After flying to Lake Van with Alev, Ari, and myself, she will rendezvous with an American Air Force pilot and co-pilot. They will be flying a MH-60G Pave Hawk helicopter based at Incirlik Air Base on the Mediterranean Sea in south central Anatolia."

Alev added, "My superiors obtained one-time special permission from Turkish government officials for the pilot to fly across our nation's air space during this vital mission."

Pat continued, "They will fly at low altitudes over northern Iraq, and cross over the Zagros Mountains into Iran through isolated mountain passes. Zivah will be inserted into the foothills west of Isfahan. Her contact, Farah, will meet her there and then drive her to the city in an old Iranian-made Paykan sedan."

"Farah translates to *Cheerful*, and I believe she will live up to her name. She definitely has a ready smile," Zivah offered.

Pat then announced, "We will communicate with Langley and each other within Iran only by sending short, encrypted text messages with BlackBerry satellite phones equipped with GPS. We will utilize the U.S. Air Force satellite communications system recently developed by Lockheed Martin. The new system is called Advanced Extremely High Frequency, or AEHF, and our messages will be protected and untraceable by the enemy. Just our code names will be used throughout the operation. We'll also use code names for the various locations." He handed out location code lists and maps of Iran, and then continued,

"Memorize them, and then cross-shred your lists and maps."

Pointing at his chest, Pat continued, "Christian and Jewish religious medals, such as my Saint Christopher and Zivah's and Ari's Star of David, won't be taken on the mission. Pseudonym identification and passports will be issued to everyone and no other ID will be taken into Iran." He cautioned his team, "Our respective agencies issued directives stating they will disavow knowledge of our mission if any of us are caught by the Iranians. So, don't get caught!"

All of the operatives agreed to carry easy to conceal, folding-stock UZI 9-millimeter submachine guns with noise suppressors for the covert mission. Pat really likes the lightweight 7-3/4-pound sub-gun, and the 40-round magazines are certainly essential during covert operations. He is very proficient in accurately placing 3-round full-automatic bursts with the folding-stock UZI, and one-inch groups at seven meters are not uncommon for him. With its 1,300 feet per second muzzle velocity, and 600-round-per-second rate of fire, this weapon is certainly awesome for close-quarters combat. He also likes the single-shot and full-auto selector switch feature on the UZI. Pat rationalized for his team, "Sure, there are more modern sub-guns . . . some with three-round burst selector switches. However, the UZI has proved to be a reliable weapon for military service over the years, and all of us are accomplished shooters with it." The other team members nodded in assent.

The operatives would also carry their personal pistols and silencers during the mission. Pat decided to carry a Glock 19, compact, 9-millimeter double-action semi-auto pistol. Therefore, as with the other operatives, his pistol ammo would then be interchangeable with his submachine gun, which will provide a definite tactical advantage. Like his Walther PPK, the Glock would be equipped with a

Crimson Trace Lasergrip sight. Moreover, the fifteen-round Glock magazine would add another tactical advantage over the Walther's six-round .380 magazine.

Pat told the group, "The Persian Caper will not be a walk in the park, because our targets are protected by the notorious Iranian Revolutionary Guards Corps . . . also known as the *Pasdaran*. We will observe and verify the nuclear research sites using Micro Aerial Vehicles. The CIA's Directorate of Science and Technology developed these bumblebee-size MAVs in conjunction with the U.S. military. Guided remotely by us, using notebook computers, several of the MAVs can fly into the sites undetected. They will take photographs, record conversations, and document exact GPS strike coordinates. We will also take still photos of the sites. Then, we will transmit the collected data and photos directly to Langley. Once the sites are confirmed, their coordinates determined, and we are safely out of the strike zones, our joint agencies will decide which actions to take. If they do decide to destroy the nuclear sites, we believe Iran will be less likely to declare a Holy War because Islamic, Jewish, and Christian nations will have jointly participated in the attacks."

Pat and Zivah shared a bottle of local Doluca white wine the first evening of the conference, and Pat thought, *Now, this is a woman I may want to spend the rest of my life with!* "We'll have to do this again, Zivah, after the mission is complete."

"Yes. I would like that." *Alev doesn't stand too much of a chance with Patrick after tonight!* Zivah reasoned, *At least not during this conference.*

They both felt a strong connection that may have been more than merely primal urges. After the conference ended, Pat and Zivah embraced, then exchanged knowing glances and smiles suggesting that they would reunite when the dangerous mission was over. Pat contemplated, *If we survive.*

The five operatives split up and left the island separately. Pat took a horse-drawn carriage directly to the ferry slip, because automotive vehicles are banned on the island. He hopped aboard the last Istanbul-bound ferry of the day.

The vessel glided across the Sea of Marmara and headed toward the Bosporus strait. With the wind and sea spray in his face at the bow of the vessel, Pat sensed someone watching him. Casually turning toward the cabin, he eyed the passengers one by one. Nobody looked suspicious and he did not recognize anyone, so he turned and faced the sea again. However, he now had a grip on his Walther and was ready for action. *No sense taking chances*, he reasoned. His encounters with Zivah took over Pat's thoughts and he relaxed his grip on the handgun.

As the ferry entered the strait and cruised past the Tower of Leander islet, Pat again sensed that someone was watching him. Glancing around the deck, he spotted a husky, light-complexioned man with a sharp-featured ruddy face peeking around a corner of the main cabin. *He looks Russian, perhaps SVR*, Pat thought. The man suddenly disappeared, and Pat did not see him again during the rest of the boat trip.

CHAPTER TWO: INSERTIONS

Day One: Viper Leader, Copperhead, Asp, Cobra

Pat pointed out the window and exclaimed, "Zivah, look, Mount Ararat!" The majestic, snow-capped 16,945-foot mountain loomed four times higher than the altitude of their Learjet. Christian and Jew alike were in awe of the Old Testament site. They both visualized Noah's Ark stranded high on the slopes, with the hand-hewn cypress wood vessel preserved in ice and snow over the millenniums. Thrilled by the scene, Pat thought, *I felt the same warm glow and excitement the last time I saw Mount Ararat.*

Pat, Zivah, Alev, and Ari had boarded an OHD Learjet 60 XR at the Istanbul International Airport. The sun was trying to peek through the fog as the jet's wheels retracted. The pilot banked the plane and headed east across the Bosporus. Then they rose out of the pea-soup fog and were greeted by a colorful sunrise. Pat sent a text message to Langley, "*wheels up at location alpha. viper leader, copperhead, asp, cobra.*"

Zivah was sitting just across the aisle from Pat. She suddenly jumped up, stepped across the aisle, leaned over Pat while pointing out the window and remarked, "Look at the sun's rays glistening on the beautiful Black Sea, Patrick." To ensure future repeats of Pat's affections, she rubbed her firm breasts against his muscular bicep.

Pat looked out at the huge, dark body of water and whispered, "Lovely, Zivah, but you're going to get me all excited, and this is a small plane!" Nonetheless, Zivah's

22

attention boosted Pat's ego. He is certainly enamored with her, and contemplated, *There will be another time, my dear Zivah!*

She smiled demurely, returned to her seat, and glanced at Alev as she mused, *Lady, he's all mine!*

Green with envy, Alev glared at Zivah from her seat and murmured, "Humph."

A flight attendant served demitasse cups of strong, sweetened Turkish coffee and fresh *baklava* dripping with honey as the plane flew just north of Ankara. Enjoying the tasty pastry, and the flavor and aroma of the coffee, Pat philosophically told Zivah, "Ah! Food for a God!" Zivah nodded in agreement, as she savored a mouthful of the delightful *baklava*.

They flew the length of Asian Turkey, over a barren plateau ringed by mountains. Pat could see Ankara, the capital of Turkey, to the south as they flew by the large metropolitan area. The rest of the country looked like desolate wasteland as they headed east.

The pilot banked the plane just after they observed Mount Ararat. Then Pat spotted huge Lake Van with its salty blue waters sparkling in the morning sun. He could also see the reddish 10th century Church of the Holy Cross standing tall on Akdamar Island as they descended to land at Van Airport. The 775-mile flight took about two hours.

Pat and Zivah both said "*Ciao*" and embraced for a few seconds when they disembarked. Pat sent a text message to Langley with his BlackBerry, *"viper leader, copperhead, asp, and cobra at location bravo."* After stowing their weapons in secret compartments underneath their waiting vehicle, Pat and Alev climbed into the Iranian-made Samand automobile and drove toward town. Ari's contact, Sadar, greeted him, and the two headed south toward Iraq in a Land Rover. Zivah's Air Force pilot was standing by with a

Pave Hawk helicopter engine warmed-up and the rotor blades turning. She jogged over to the aircraft.

Day One continued: Viper Leader, Copperhead

Pat drove by the ancient Uratu Citadel and passed through Old Van. He then headed east, past fertile farmlands, toward Kapikoy on the Iran border 50 miles away. Alev made her play for Pat during the drive. She unbuttoned her blouse to expose her well-developed bare breasts and boldly asked, with a sultry look, "What do you think, Patrick?"

"Nice boobs. Now button-up before we reach the border." Alev pouted during the remainder of the drive to the Turkey-Iran border.

The Kapikoy-Razi crossing went relatively smooth, as the Islamic Republic of Iran Border Guards were more interested in Alev's voluptuous figure than they were in Pat or the vehicle. Perhaps his *"Salaam, hale shoma chetowre?"* greeting in Persian, as well as his Eastern Turkey attire and the two-day unshaven facial stubble helped. The border guards reviewed the Samand registration and the operatives' bogus passports, gave the vehicle a cursory inspection, and then let them pass through into Iran.

Once through the border inspection station, Alev donned a black full-length *chador* over her Turkish skirt and blouse so she would not attract more attention. It was also very important that she conform to Iran's strict *hijab* dress code for women. *Hijab* requires clothing that covers the entire body with only the hands and face visible. After the current president took office, Iran began a severe nation-wide crackdown on women who did not follow the strict Islamic dress code. Punishments include public beatings with batons and incarcerations, so Alev was not taking any chances. Pat thought, *I guess that's the end of Alev's impromptu sexual displays, at least for a while!*

They then continued east on an almost impassable secondary road through the rugged, barren, snow-capped Zagros Mountains toward Khoy. Just past the mountain village of Qotur, they spotted a military vehicle coming toward them a few miles down the mountain road. Pat hollered, "I hope they didn't see us," as he immediately pulled into a narrow canyon and stopped just out of sight of the road. Pat and Alev jumped out of the Samand, retrieved their hidden weapons from under the vehicle, and readied the UZIs for a firefight. However, the Iranians did not spot them, and the military vehicle went past the canyon and on up the mountain road.

"That was certainly a close call!" Alev exclaimed.

"That it was . . . that it was."

The two operatives snacked on bread and cheese to pass the time as dark storm clouds passed overhead. Pat said, "I pray it doesn't snow until we get out of these mountains!" They were back on the road about fifteen minutes later when they thought the patrol was out of sight.

While driving through the mountains, Pat reflected on his History of Iran studies at the University of Tehran. "Alev, did you know that Darius the Great's Persian Army, and Alexander the Great's Greek Army, may have marched along this very same mountain road centuries before Jesus Christ was born?

"Yes, I suppose they did. Wasn't that before the prophet Mohammed was born?"

Pat merely nodded and pondered, *Is Alev really that dense?* The drive from Khoy to Tabriz on a primary highway was effortless, except for an occasional flock of sheep in the middle of the road. They passed through the villages of Marand and Sufian without attracting too much attention, although a few curious locals did glance at their vehicle as they whizzed by.

Pat and Alev were soon entering a lovely valley lined with red-hued mountains to the north and west, which reminded Pat of Sedona, Arizona. Alev exclaimed, "I love the natural beauty of this area."

Tabriz, in the heart of the Persian Azerbaijan region, appeared below them as they descended down from the high mountains. It was a warm, sunny day in Tabriz, the 4,600-foot elevation city visited by Marco Polo in 1294. Pat offered, "The weather's just like the last time I visited this beautiful valley." The 175-mile trip from Van took nearly six hours.

They stopped at Alev's cousin's villa on the outskirts of the city just as a *muezzin's* call to prayer, for the third of the five daily *namez*, echoed from the local mosque minaret. Alev jumped out of the car, dashed to embrace her family members, and yelled, "I've missed you!" The servants opened the villa gates wide to let Pat drive the Samand onto the grounds, where he parked the vehicle under a huge white mulberry tree. Then Alev introduced him to her cousin, Nader, and his wife Gesoo. Once inside the seclusion of Nader's home, Alev threw off her *chador*, again displaying her erotic figure. She yelled, "I hate this wretched thing!" Her fervent exclamation drew chuckles from Pat, Nader, and Gesoo.

Pat noticed the colorful handmade Persian carpet, and the exquisite material covering the overstuffed furniture in the living room. He addressed Nader and Gesoo, "You have a lovely home. It is just as I remember the classic Persian home when I was stationed in Tehran many years ago." He then sent Langley and the rest of the team a text message with his BlackBerry, *"viper leader and copperhead safe at location charlie."*

In the typical Persian tradition, Nader and his family were friendly, gracious hosts. Gesoo served the national dish, *chelo kebab*, for dinner. They sat crossed-legged on a Persian carpet in the middle of the kitchen, and *khanom* Gesoo deftly broke a raw egg and gently placed the yolk on top of everyone's huge mound of saffron spiced boiled white rice. Pat recognized the pungent aroma of the saffron as Gesoo placed slices of sweet onions and marinated, grilled lamb kebabs alongside the rice. It seemed like too much for him to eat. However, it was a long, tiring day, and he was hungry enough to eat it all, which he did, after telling Gesoo, "*Merci*, Madame." Besides, it would have been rude if he did not completely finish the meal.

When they finished their *chelo kebabs*, Gesoo gave Pat and Alev generous helpings of delicious, crispy, burnt rice, which was scraped from the bottom of the rice kettle. Gesoo said, with a broad smile, "For our special guests." Pat remembered that Persians loved burnt rice, and he felt honored to be served such a large portion of the treat.

After dinner, Gesoo served hot *chahee*. The fragrant Caspian tealeaves were steeped in a small teapot atop an ornate, charcoal-fueled silver samovar until the tea was extra strong. She poured the tea into petite gold-rimmed glasses, and then diluted the strong tea with hot water from the samovar tap. Sugar cubes were passed around to hold between the front teeth while sipping the tea. As Pat placed a cube between his teeth, Nader remarked, "I see you know our customs."

Pat recalled perfecting the technique when he was stationed in Tehran and replied, "Yes, Nader. I will never forget the Persian customs I learned when I lived in Iran years ago."

He used the Middle Eastern squat toilet before retiring, which was merely a hole in the floor with two footpads for correct positioning, and a water pitcher instead of toilet paper for personal hygiene. Pat mused, *I remember the correct procedure for using the archaic facility very well from my tour of duty days in Tehran. And, I'll never forget the cardinal rules of always using the left hand for the cleansing procedure and never using that hand to eat with or to shake hands.*

Pat received text messages from Zivah and Ari that evening, indicating they were inserted in Iran. He was given a blanket and offered a pile of Persian carpets and the typical rolled pillow to sleep on. The handmade carpets, piled several feet high, were part of the family's wealth. Feeling secure in Nader's home, Pat slept like a baby the entire night and had pleasant dreams about Zivah. Alev slept with Nader's daughter.

Day Two: Viper Leader, Copperhead

Pat and Alev were up before dawn the next morning, and Gesoo served warm, tasty *nan-e-bahr-bahr-ee*, tangy goat cheese to eat with the thick flatbread, and hot *chahee* for breakfast. Nader translates to *Rare*, and Pat said, "Nader, you are indeed a rare friend." Alev donned her *chador* and they departed in the Samand at daybreak with Pat driving. They went through the city, past the majestic 15th century Blue Mosque and the attractive, well-kept University of Tabriz campus. About six miles out of town, Pat drove by Shahgoli Park, a lovely verdant oasis and the location of an ancient Qajar dynasty summer palace. He exclaimed, "I'm very fond of this city."

"I can see why. Even with more than a million residents, it is a beautiful city. You know, Tabriz was occupied by the Russians in 1826, and again in 1941," Alev offered. They continued eastward to Bostanabad, and then turned off the Tabriz-Tehran Highway and headed east toward the Caspian Sea on the Astara-Tabriz Highway.

The two of them made good time on the secondary paved highway, because there was very little vehicular traffic and they did not encounter roadblocks. Although, they did meet a few horse drawn hay wagons along the way. While driving through the town of Sarab nestled at the base of volcanic Mount Sabalan, Alev remarked, "Sarab is one of the oldest settlements in Iran. And this area has many mineral hot springs." Pat nodded and continued driving on to Ardabil. Passing through the town, Alev said, "Archaeologists recently found evidence of human habitat in this area dating back to the 16th century BC." Again, Pat nodded an acknowledgement.

As they drove through Ardabil, Pat pointed out the window and remarked, "That looks like a Christian church. It has a cross on top."

"Yes, that is the Armenian Church of Maryam Muqaddas."

"Oh, Saint Mary's." There was snow on the highest peaks as they crossed over the bare, brown-colored Talish Mountains. Pat whimsically thought, *Now, that looks like chocolate ice cream topped with whipped cream!*

The largest landlocked body of water on earth, the beautiful Caspian Sea, greeted them as they dropped down out of the mountains into the verdant *jangal*, or jungle, of the Caspian basin and headed for Astara. Pat informed Alev, "This border town, adjacent to Azerbaijan, is where a column of Russian tanks lined up at the international boundary in 1978. They were ready to invade Iran during the pending revolution. Essentially, the U.S.S.R. wanted a year-round warm-water port on the Persian Gulf for their Cold War exploits. It seems the communist leaders in Moscow believed that invading Iran while it was under turmoil would provide such a port. We made sure the Russians changed their minds about that!"

"Patrick, this town is certainly a prime location for smuggling Russian vodka into abstemious Iran, and perhaps cigarettes."

"Yes, and I suppose many other illicit goods."

Pat and Alev were hot and sticky from the extremely high humidity in the basin by the time they arrived at Astara, where they were stopped at an impromptu Ansar-e-Hezbollah roadblock. The Hezbollah, or Party of God, was formed at the time of the Ayatollah Ruhollah Khomeini Islamic Revolution. Members fanatically follow Islamic tenets, and they wear easily recognizable black and white Palestinian-style headscarves.

With a Russian-made full-auto, AK-47 assault rifle pointed at Pat and Alev, one of the *Hezbollahi* guards ordered, "Halt! Papers please," in *Farsi*. Pat handed him their passports, and the guard studied them thoroughly. Fearing the worst, Pat was ready to open up on the guards with his UZI.

However, Alev smiled demurely and said in Persian, "Please, sir, my husband and I are merely traveling from Tabriz to Chalus. We have business affairs to attend to at the bazaar."

Alev's fast-talking, and Pat's convincing role as a traveling Turkish businessman, prevented an armed confrontation that may have ended their involvement in The Persian Caper. Pat's three-day stubble may have also helped, as all of the *Hezbollahi* sported unshaven facial growths, and his attire masked his distinctive occidental features. The guards merely glanced in the vehicle and waved them through.

Pat said, "*Khoda Hafez*" as they left the roadblock, and he received non-committal nods from the *Hezbollahi* for the Go With God farewell. He thought, *Whew! That was our second close call in two days.*

"You know, Patrick, Iran is really a military state today, just like North Korea."

Pat nodded and said, "Yep, it sure is." The two operatives headed south and followed the coastline, with the only real greenbelt region in Iran to their right, and the Caspian Sea to their left. They drove through the seaside towns of Hashtpar and Bandar-e-Anzai, which was called Bandar-e-Pahlavi when Pat was there before the revolution, and then into the large city of Rasht. There was another checkpoint in the center of town, but they managed to avoid it by taking *kuches,* or back alleys across town.

Pat and Alev continued in the direction of Chalus, passing by rich, verdant tea and rice growing farms and through the villages of Lahijan and Langrud. Alev offered, "Lahijan was the first location in Persia to have tea plantations, and it currently has the largest area of tea cultivation in the country."

A red fox crossed the road in front of them and Pat slammed on the brakes. He exclaimed, "That was close."

Alev nodded in agreement and replied, "I would have hit the beast." They continued down the road and drove through the fishing and agricultural town of Rudsar.

Entering the town, Pat advised, "Alev, don't drink the water here! The dense green woods and lush cultivated fields are misleading, because Ramsar has the highest levels of natural radiation in the world. And the spas at the hot springs have high concentrations of radium, so don't skinny dip there." Alev laughed until her side hurt.

The next town was Tonekabon, known as Shahsavar before the Islamic Revolution. Just down the road from Tonekabon, they passed by an Armenian Christian compound on the beach side of the road. Pat declared, "The Armenian Christians are allowed to make and drink wine within the high walls of this compound, and the women are allowed to wear swimsuits while sunbathing and swimming with the men. Both actions are forbidden throughout the rest of this stern Islamic nation."

Alev, shouted gleefully, "And no damn *chadors* in there!" Arriving at Chalus, she directed, "Patrick, turn south on the Chalus-Karaj Highway and head toward the Alborz Mountains." After Pat drove a few miles through the fertile tea-growing area, she said, "Now turn onto this side road on the left and park behind that white stone farmhouse." This was Hamideh's home, Alev's contact. She immediately sent a text message to Langley and the rest of the team, *"copperhead inserted at location foxtrot."* The 325-mile journey from Tabriz took less than eight hours.

The family provided the two hungry travelers with a simple meal of *nan-e-lavash*, goat cheese to eat with the thin flatbread, charcoal-grilled Caspian salmon, and hot *chahee*.

Day Two continued: Viper Leader

Pat's contact, Hossein, arrived at Hamideh's home that evening in an old maroon Mercedes-Benz. Alev gave Pat a hug, a peck on both cheeks, and a knowing wink. Pat said, "*Kal*, Alev!"

She nodded appreciation for the Turkish goodbye and responded with, "*Kal!* Patrick."

He jumped into the driver's seat, and they headed for Tehran. Just south of the tea growing plantations, Hossein exclaimed, "That's the main gate to the Chalus underground nuclear weapons development facility on the right. It's buried deep into the base of that tall snow-capped mountain."

"Well, Hossein, Alev certainly has her hands full trying to get close to that site!" Pat remembered the treacherous, hair-raising, two-lane Chalus-Karaj Highway very well, because he drove it many times while stationed at the

American Embassy in Tehran. He especially remembered the mile-long, one-way, one-lane tunnel going through the mountain near the summit in the Alborz Mountains. Tunnel traffic was controlled with red and green traffic lights at each entrance, and he always prayed there was not an impatient Iranian driver coming toward him at high speed when he got the green light to enter. During the trip this day, Pat was startled when three cars abreast came toward him on a curve, one of them straddling the centerline! Only his fast reflexes and nerves of steel prevented a tragedy, as he expertly maneuvered to the side of the road and stopped inches from a 1,000-foot drop-off. He yelled, "Wow! That was scary."

"Iran sure has some aggressive drivers, Pat."

"I see that not much has changed since I last drove here." On the other side of the mountain, they proceeded along the Karaj River, past Karaj Lake and Dam, and then down toward the desert city of Karaj.

Hossein was stopped at an Ansar-e-Hezbollah roadblock in the city on his trip from Tehran earlier that day. Therefore, he told Pat, "We need to detour through the desert to avoid a checkpoint." Guided by Hossein, Pat skirted around the town on dirt tracks, which were more suitable for camel travel than for a Mercedes. Of course, they did frighten a few lumbering camels during the detour, and the beasts slobbered on the car when they tried to bite it.

As they entered the capital city, familiar sights, such as Tehran's Mehrabad International Airport and the Shahyad Arya Monument, greeted Pat like an old friend. Hossein offered, "The Shahyad Monument is now called Azadi Tower and Square, thanks to the revolution."

"I understand." Seeing the famous monument, built by the Shah in 1971 to commemorate the 2,500-year anniversary of Persia, brought back bittersweet memories

33

for Pat of the last time he was in Tehran. "Hossein, the smog and traffic is much worse than I remember when I was here before."

Hossein remarked, "It is, and traffic gets worse every year. Take the old Tarasht Highway north, Pat." He did, and then turned left onto Vanak Parkway.

Pat shuddered as they went past the drab, sprawling old SAVAK prison in the Evin district, and he recalled the horror stories of torture within its gray stone walls under the Shah's regime. "Hossein, I remember the daily sweeps for listening devices that SAVAK agents, posing as cleaning crews, would place in the American Embassy and the nearby American Consulate offices at night. We frequently found them in our conference room thermostats. I bet things haven't changed much at Evin Prison."

"Not a bit, Pat. Other than it is now a VEVAK prison. We still live in a police state, and it is still cruel and inhumane in Evin! That is where an Israeli F-4 fighter jet pilot has been imprisoned and tortured since 1986, after Hezbollah in Lebanon captured him. Iran supports that terrorist group, as well as the Hamas terrorist group in Palestine."

Passing by the tall, stately Esteghlal Hotel just past Evin Prison, Pat asked, "Wasn't that the Hilton Hotel before the revolution?"

"Yes, and I recall going to the Hilton with you for an American Embassy Christmas banquet in 1978. Do you remember the exquisite ice carvings and sculptured butter animals?"

"Of course I do. Those were enjoyable days, even during the Martial Law period." They continued on to Hossein's villa, located on a *kuche* off Zafaranieh Street in the Taj Rish district of northern Tehran. His servants opened the gate on the narrow side street and Pat parked the

Mercedes behind the villa's ten-foot-tall wall. The 100-mile trip from Chalus took nearly 3 hours. Pat immediately sent Langley and his team a text message, *"viper leader inserted at location delta."* He also received a text message from Logan that evening indicating he was inserted in Iran. Pat felt satisfied that the entire team was in place and ready to carry out their vital mission. Hossein's *khanom*, Azar, served the travelers delicious, aromatic *ghosht-en-khor-est* lamb stew, *nan-e-lavash*, white mulberries, and hot *chahee* for a late night supper. Pat dreamed about being with Zivah throughout the night.

Day One continued: Asp

Ari and Sadar continued southward, with Sadar driving the Land Rover. They went through desolate foothills and stopped at the villages of Hosup and Baskale, where Sadar greeted his relatives and obtained information on road conditions and checkpoints for their drive through the Kurdish region of Iraq. The two of them continued down the road and passed through the villages of Sivclan and Yuksekova. The next stop was at Begor near the Iraqi border. More of Sadar's relatives provided additional information on road conditions and security checkpoints ahead. They drove down a mountainous dirt track, crossed the border into the Republic of Iraq, and continued cross-country toward the village of Zibar.

The drive to Zibar was uneventful because this was a distinctly Kurdistan region, and the going would be smooth until they got to Halajabah and the Iran border. As they passed by the Stone Age Shanidar Cave, Sadar remarked, "This is where archeologists found 60,000 year-old remains of a baby preserved in the desert sands."

Ari responded, "That was more than 56,000 years before Abraham was born at Ur in the south. That's really incredible!"

Heading southeast, the duo drove through the towns of Rawanduz, Raniyah, and 7,000 year-old Zarzi. They were stopped at a Kurd roadblock as they entered the town of As Sulaymaniyah in the oil-rich region. However, Sadar knew some of the guards and they greeted each other in Kurdish. After Sadar convinced them that Ari was a Hebrew, not an Arab, they were allowed to pass through.

They drove through Arbat village and into the city of Halabajah. "Ari, this is where Saddam Hussein's Iraqi military forces attacked the Kurds with mustard gas and nerve agents in March of 1988. The reports said 5,000 were killed, and another 10,000 were injured during the horrific attack."

"I read the intelligence reports on that savage attack. It was a horrible ethnic genocide!"

They headed east on a dirt track toward Iran and crossed over the border. Sadar drove into a narrow canyon in the central Zagros Mountains and followed the rocky bottom of a dry *wadi*. "Ari, this sandy, rock-strewn, dry streambed will take us through a secret pass that's been used for centuries by the Kurds to go back and forth between Mesopotamia and Persia freely without being noticed. It's a popular route with smugglers."

"It's amazing that the Arabs and the Persians have never found this clandestine route."

Sadar nodded. "Not long ago, three American hikers, a woman and two men, were captured above this pass by an Iranian border patrol. They are still detained at the notorious Evin Prison in Tehran."

"Sadar, the Iranian government claims the hikers are spies, and that they purposely crossed over into Iran from Iraq. But, I don't believe they did. I think the Iranian Border Patrol seized them on Iraqi soil. I heard that the woman was released on $500,000 bail recently. She is back in the states now."

"I also heard about that. I wonder if the government will release the two men now."

Ari merely shrugged his shoulders.

Emerging near Sanandaj in Iran, they skirted around the mountain town by driving down another dry streambed surrounded by woods, because Sadar's relatives had warned him that there might be an Iranian military roadblock in central Sanandaj. On the other side of the town, Sadar drove out of the streambed onto a secondary paved road, and eventually onto the Sanandaj Highway. He then headed east toward Hamadan while commenting, "My sister lives in Sanandaj. It is the capital of the Iranian province of Kurdistan and the people speak Sorani Kurdish. Most of them are Sunnis."

The two operatives went through the villages of Dehgolan and Qorveh in the Kurdish region without incident. Women alongside the road wore colorful, airy ethnic clothing, yet followed the strict *hijab* dress code of not showing bare arms or legs. "Ari, Kurdish women are allowed to wear their tribal clothing out here in the countryside, but they usually don black *chadors* when in the big cities."

Sadar proceeded into ancient Hamadan, the oldest existing Persian city. After driving past the location of the tombs of Esther and Mordecai in the center of town, Ari gave directions to Sadar on how to get to his great-uncle Abraham's villa on the north side of the city. On arrival, he sent a text message to Langley and the team, "*asp inserted at location golf.*" The 500-mile trek took about fourteen hours. Abraham welcomed Ari and Sadar, and then gave them something to eat before they retired for the evening. Before falling asleep, Ari reminisced about his past relationship with Zivah, *I really liked her. It's too bad our strong personalities clashed and it didn't work out for us.*

Day One continued: Adder

At Istanbul, Logan boarded a Turkish Airlines jet heading for Amman, Jordan. Wheels were up at dawn. While the jetliner gained altitude, he sent Langley a text message, *adder departing location alpha.* The flight took him across the Bosporus strait and western Anatolia in Turkey, the eastern tip of Cyprus in the dark-blue Mediterranean Sea, northern Israel, the West Bank of Palestine, and then into Amman, the capital of the Hashemite Kingdom of Jordan. The 735-mile trip took just over 2 hours.

He had an hour layover at the Amman International Terminal before the Kuwait Airlines connecting flight left for Kuwait City. This leg of the journey took him across the breadth of the northern part of the Kingdom of Saudi Arabia, where Logan could see only golden sand dunes in the scorched desert below. The 740-mile flight to the State of Kuwait took about two hours and fifteen minutes.

Logan's contact, Farhad, was waiting for him at the Kuwait International Terminal. They exchanged *"As salam'alakoom"* greetings in Arabic so they wouldn't attract attention, and then headed for the taxi stand in front of the terminal. The cab driver dropped them off at the fishing fleet wharf, where Farhad had a rather old Arab fishing *dhow* fueled up and waiting for them. The traditional wooden vessel, a widely recognized icon of the Arab culture, was selected because it would be inconspicuous and more likely to slip past Iraqi and Iranian patrol boats as they were en route to Ahvaz, Iran. Farhad advised, "As you requested, I stocked the boat with an UZI and Beretta for you, an AK-47 for me, and extra loaded magazines for all of the weapons."

38

"Great, I knew I could rely on you."

They cruised across the northeast corner of the Persian Gulf for fifty miles. About the time they entered the Shatt al-Arab, on the Iraq side of the river, an Iraqi patrol boat pulled along side the *dhow*. Dressed in Arab *djellaba* desert robes and *keffiyah* headdresses, and speaking fluent Arabic, Logan and Farhad tried to convince the Iraqis they were merely local fishermen. Finally, Farhad shouted, *"Allah o Akbar."* The God is Great salutation satisfied the patrol boat captain and he waved them on.

The half-mile wide murky waterway was lined with date palm groves on the Iraq and Iran shorelines. They went past Abadan, a large city island on the Iran side of the river 33 miles upstream from the gulf, and two Iranian gunboats followed them the length of the island. Logan said, "They appear to be ready to challenge us if we wander across the invisible border in the middle of the river."

Farhad nodded an affirmative and waved at the patrol boats, as he replied to Logan, "We will have to cross over to Iran after they leave." The Iranian patrols gave up on them as they went past the northwest tip of Abadan. One set a course downstream toward the Persian Gulf, and the other one headed upstream toward Khorramshar at full speed.

When both patrol boats were out of sight, Farhad piloted the *dhow* straight across the Shatt al-Arab to the Iran side. He felt more comfortable then, because he was now in his native country. They continued six miles upstream to the ancient port city of Khorramshar at the confluence of the Shatt al-Arab and the Karun River. Farhad said, "I understand that the United States Army built this modern port during World War II."

"That they did, old chap, that they did." Pretending to fish, Logan and Farhad cruised slowly up the Karun River toward Ahvaz 65 miles upstream on the only navigable river in Iran. They spotted a few shark dorsal fins gliding by the boat. Logan said, "I saw them bloody suckers swimming under the White Bridge the last time I was in Ahvaz."

As they went past Darkhovin, a date palm oasis village on the east shore, Logan remarked, "Farhad, do you know that there is a uranium enrichment site here?"

"No. I am surprised that I did not know about it. Like many other nuclear locations, it must be a secret the government does not want us to know about."

They then entered a winding narrow canyon. When they finally emerged out of the canyon, the two travelers immediately spotted a pall of oil refinery smoke hanging over the city of Ahvaz. The oil and natural gas wells were too numerous to count as they cruised toward the dirty, drab city center, and burning excess natural gas spewed out of tall smokestacks.

Farhad tied up the *dhow* just past the White Bridge. With their weapons concealed under their desert robes, they walked a few blocks to Farhad's uncle's home near the Ahvaz Bazaar. While strolling down the side streets, Logan noted that the local women wore the same type of black *chadors* that were worn in Tehran and Qom. However, most of the men were dressed in Arab *djellabas* and *keffiyahs*.

Farhad's ten-year-old black Mercedes was parked behind the wall of his Uncle Ahmad's home. Logan was anxious to get on the road, but Ahmad insisted it was too late in the day to drive down the desolate highway and graciously offered them a meal and lodging for the night. "As my guest, you must eat our delicious *morg polow*," exclaimed Ahmad. Totally exhausted, Logan accepted the kind offer and enjoyed the rice and chicken dish. Then he sent a text message to Langley and the team, "*adder safe at location india.*"

Day Two continued: Adder

Logan and Farhad headed southeast in the Mercedes before dawn the next morning. They drove through Khalfabad, Behbahan, and Dogonbahan while crossing the southern Zagros Mountains. The sun was rising across the desolate desert as they dropped down out of the barren, rugged mountains and spotted lovely Shiraz.

They traveled along the tree-lined streets of "The City of Roses, Wine and Poets" before the locals were stirring. While passing by the beautiful Hafez and Saadi monuments, Farhad remarked, "This is where the Princes of Persian Poets are buried."

Logan responded, "I visited the sites years ago when I was here. I also sampled the excellent red Shiraz wine made in this region then. Of course, that was before the revolution, when the Shah allowed the sale and consumption of alcoholic beverages in Iran." As they passed by the Armenian sector of Sarjooy, Logan commented, "I see the tall steeple of the Christian Church. I remember enjoying the beauty of the lovely Safavid period paintings and ornamental plaster work inside the church."

"Yes, it is a beautiful church."

The two headed north from Shiraz and passed through Marvdasht. They entered a barren plain surrounded by purplish-hued cliffs and drove by 2,500-year-old Persepolis, the City of the Persians. Towering columns of intricately carved stone reached out of the ruins toward the sky, and Logan remarked, "I recall exploring the remains of the ancient city built by Cyrus the Great during my last trip to this region."

"I also have been here before, while I was studying the history of my country. Persepolis *is* quite old and interesting."

Further up the highway, they drove through the desert village of Dehbid. A few miles north, at Surmag, they headed east toward Yazd on a secondary road. After driving through Faragheh, Abarqu, and a few tiny mud villages, they spotted the tall, square wind funnel cooling towers used for venting the blistering desert heat from the interiors of the buildings in Yazd. "Those are *badgirs*, Logan, and they are very common in the desert communities. You may know, Yazd is the driest major city in Iran."

"Yes, I do. The cross vents at the top of the *badgers* catch the winds and funnel them downwards into a large container filled with water. Then the winds pick up moisture from the water, blow it through the building, and push hot air out the windows. It's quite an ancient, but very effective cooling system."

The large sand-colored Jami Mosque, with its colorful yellow, turquoise, white, and black ceramic tile roof, stood out in the middle of the drab-looking mud and clay desert city. To avoid possible checkpoints in the large town, Farhad skirted around Yazd by driving on the dirt tracks of the ancient Silk Road at the edge of *Dasht-e-Kavir*, the Great Salt Desert. "Marco Polo rode camels on these very same caravan tracks when he visited Yadz in 1250 AD. I also explored this region extensively while going to college here. This is the largest desert wilderness area in Iran," Farhad offered.

Logan replied, "I rode camels out into the Great Salt Desert to the east of here, just for the experience. My Iranian friends said I was crazy, because they would never do that. 'Only foreigners ride camels in the desert!' they claimed."

Farhad drove north through Aqda, Nain, and Neyestanak. Just before entering the desert community of Ardestan, located in the southern foothills of the stark Karkas Mountains, they drove past huge mulberry, pomegranate, and fig orchards. "In case you are wondering, these orchards are irrigated by *qanats*, which bring water from the mountains to the arid desert."

"I know, Farhad, because I studied the hand-dug underground aqueduct systems. I also followed many of their routes during my previous travels here." After passing by the Friday Mosque, just as the *muezzin's* call to evening prayer commenced, Farhad pulled into his cousin Amir's villa and hid the Mercedes behind the tall stone wall. Logan immediately sent Langley and the team a text message, *"adder inserted at location juliet."* The 650-mile drive from Ahvaz took just less than 13 hours. He then reflected, *I'm getting too ruddy old for this kind of operation. It's time to retire and lead a tranquil life in the Scottish highlands. I can then spend leisurely hours searching for Nessie at peaceful Loch Ness, instead of searching for nuclear weapon sites in the desert of a fervent terrorist nation!*

Day One continued: Cobra

With a huge, warm smile, Zivah flashed her fictitious passport for identification and introduced herself to the helicopter crew. The young Air Force pilot responded with a strictly military, "I'm First Lieutenant Brennan, ma'am," as he eyed the petite, charming woman hopping aboard his aircraft.

The second lieutenant co-pilot grinned as he waved at her, and said, "Joe, ma'am." Zivah settled down between the two 7.62-millimeter mini-guns mounted in the cabin's side windows and prepared to operate them if necessary.

They lifted off and headed south, flying low to stay out of hostile as well as friendly radar. It was not long before they were across the Iraq border and heading down the Tigris valley. The pilot followed the river at 184 miles per hour, the aircraft's top cruising speed. He explained, "I hope to surprise al-Qaida insurgents and Tehran-backed Shiite militias, thereby preventing them from having enough time to shoulder and aim their rocket launchers as we zoom by."

He also kept in touch with Iraqi and Kurdish military forces in the region so they would not be hit by friendly fire.

Zivah had a bite to eat at the snack bar while the aircraft was refueled at Balad U.S. Air Force Base near Baghdad. Then they flew due east toward Iran and headed into the rugged central Zagros Mountains after crossing the border. Flying low at top speed through narrow canyons to avoid detection was certainly tricky. With a roller coaster ride sensation in her stomach, Zivah yelled, "This is thrilling, Lieutenant Brennan."

Sporting a big grin, the pilot remarked, "I thought you'd like it!"

They soon entered the Simareh River canyon and followed it southeast. Just north of Dezful, the pilot took an easterly course and followed the canyons in the barren mountains of the isolated area. Nearing Isfahan, he stayed clear of villages and roads as much as possible. The pilot then hovered twenty feet above a small sandy beach on the Karun River in the varied earth-tone foothills of snow-capped Zard Mountain, and Zivah fast-roped down to the ground. She had performed fast-roping during previous missions, and had mastered the dangerous technique of sliding down the thick, plaited rope with gloves to protect her hands. Lieutenant Brennan and Joe lowered her gear bag, and then saluted Zivah. She responded with a big smile, a casual wave, and hollered, "*Shalom!*" The Pave Hawk pilot then headed back toward the Iraq border.

Using her GPS locater, Zivah hiked out of the river canyon toward the dirt road where she would meet her contact, Farah. Thoughts about Pat kept popping up in her mind, *I wonder if we'll get together again. I really like him, maybe even love him. What would it be like to spend the rest of our lives together . . . as Jew and Christian? Would that work? Maybe I can join the Jews for Jesus movement.*

After hiking several miles in the rough, arid terrain amid rocky hillsides, she spotted Farah standing next to a dusty non-descript, cream-colored Iranian Paykan automobile. Zivah greeted her with a broad smile and an enthusiastic, "Farah! *Hale shoma chetowre?*"

Farah responded with an equally enthusiastic, "Zivah! *Khoob, merci maemnum. Hale shoma chetowre?*" The two hugged and kissed each other on both cheeks in the Persian manner after their "How are you?" greetings.

Farah drove east toward Isfahan. After going through Nadjafabad, they entered the lovely desert oasis of Isfahan. She went past colorful mosques covered with blue, turquoise, and golden-hued ceramic tiles. The sparkling jewel of a city, with its bright-green tree-lined boulevards and lush parks and gardens, was certainly a welcome sight for Zivah. She commented, "I always loved the beauty of Isfahan." Farah nodded in assent and continued past Jolfa, the Armenian Christian district, then past the Forty Pillars Palace, *Chihil Sutun.* Zivah spotted a group of women, wearing colorful flower-print *chadors,* washing laundry and Persian carpets in the Zayandeh River as they crossed it on the *Si-o-se Pol.* "Farah, I see they're still washing clothing and carpets in the river."

"And, they always will. You know, the first Shah Abbas built this thirty-three arcade bridge in the 1600s, and it is one of the most famous examples of Safavid architecture. But, my people were washing carpets in the Zayandeh *Rud* long before then."

Farah pulled into her family's villa on the east side of town and parked behind the ten-foot wall surrounding her home and beautiful flower garden. The 750-mile air and land trip from Van took just over eight hours. Zivah promptly sent Langley and the team a text message, "*cobra inserted at location lima.*" Then she pensively contemplated, *I sure wish I could talk to Patrick, or at least send him a personal text message.*

CHAPTER THREE: TEHRAN

Hossein is tall, dark, and handsome. He carries his lithe 150-pound frame with confidence. Although the man traces his genealogy to pure Persian roots, he does not display the egotistical nature of many Iranian men. Moreover, he does not believe in the traditional Persian male dominance over females. These traits of his disturbed his male friends and many of them drifted away from Hossein. Along with his extended family, he practices the Shia Muslim religion.

Hossein had graduated from the University of Tehran with a Bachelor of Arts degree in the Humanities, and he is very well read. He met his future wife, Azar, a beautiful dark-haired and dark-eyed young Tehrani woman, on the university campus while she was attending archeology classes. The fifty-year-old now lives in Tehran with his wife of twenty-five years, and they are childless. His parents are deceased, and his sister lives in the United States with her American husband and two children. He has not seen his sister since she went to the States to attend the University of Southern California, where she met her future husband. Hossein's mother-in-law and father in-law live in the Chizar district of Tehran, a short distance from him and Azar.

Hossein's political leanings are toward a secular government, and he prays to Allah daily for the overthrow of the hard-core Islamic regime. As young adults, he and Patrick O'Leary were good friends while Pat was a Marine guard at the American Embassy. They met at the Iran American Society, spent a lot of time together, and thoroughly enjoyed each other's company. Therefore, Hossein was more than happy to accept his friend's offer to join him in a clandestine operation against the current Iranian government. He always dreamed about being a secret agent, and now he was going to be one. However, Azar had reservations, and she had a feeling that something dreadful might happen to her husband.

Day Three: Viper Leader

Hossein drove past the Taj Rish Bazaar, turned right onto Shariati Street, and headed south toward the city center. Pat asked, "Wasn't this street called Kurosh-e Kabir when I was stationed here?"

Hossein responded, "Yes, it was. Many streets were renamed shortly after the Khomeini Islamic Revolution ended."

There was a demonstration near the old British School grounds, and Pat asked, "What's going on here?"

"That is the Basiji Militia protesting in front of Shirin Ebadi's home and office. They are a hard-line Islamic group subordinate to and taking orders from the elite Iranian Revolutionary Guards. The Basiji paramilitary group has a long history of abusing human rights in Iran."

The militia demonstrators chanted in *Farsi*, "Death to the pen-pushing mercenary!" They tore down a sign with her name on it, and spray-painted offensive slogans on the building walls as Pat and Hossein drove by her home. The local police, some laughing with big grins on their faces, merely stood by and observed the demonstrators.

"All this violent animosity because Ebadi wrote a report that prompted the United Nations to issue a resolution calling for Iran to improve the nation's human rights performance," Pat remarked while shaking his head. "She was the first Persian, and the first Muslim woman, to win a Nobel Peace Prize. I understand that Iranian authorities recently confiscated her Peace Medal, her Legion of Honor award, and all of her files. You know, with a record of more than 1,000 people killed in Iranian-backed terrorist attacks around the world since 1979, including more than 80 assassinations of political dissidents by hit squads, Shirin Ebadi may not be around much longer either. For her safety, it's good that she's out of the country now."

Hossein nodded in agreement and said, "She is a fine human rights lawyer, an excellent judge, and she *was* teaching law at the University of Tehran. I feel sad that the government wants to silence her."

"You know, I have pleasant memories of Tehran." As they continued down the boulevard, Pat mused about the past. *I remember walking the Dowlat, Saltanatabad, Kurosh-e Kabir triangle for exercise while living here. That was quite a half-day jaunt. I see that they even changed Saltanatabad to Pasdaran Street after the revolution.* Then he said, "It seems that the combined traffic of Paris, Rome, and New York City isn't as bad as this!"

Hossein responded, "I do not know about those other cities, but the traffic and the drivers *are* bad here." He turned west on Behesti Street, then drove into the Amirabad district and headed toward the Tehran Nuclear Research Center.

Stopping in a *kuche* behind a tall office building near the research center, Hossein remarked, "This is where I rented a top floor office for us to work in."

"It looks like a good location." They took the lift to the top floor and viewed the research center from the office window. Pat could also see Mount Tuchal to the north where he hiked in the summer months, and Mount Damavand to the northeast where he liked to ski in the winter. Puffy white clouds hung over the tall, snow-capped Alborz landmarks. With a smile, he said, "This is perfect, Hossein. We can see the two main entrances facing the boulevard, as well as the delivery dock on the right side of the building."

Pat took photos of the building exterior, then remarked, "Let's set up the surveillance equipment." They opened the window and set three bumblebee-size Micro Aerial Vehicles on the sill. Pat booted his notebook computer and they were ready. "As the staff members come and go, we'll send one MAV into each of the main entrances, and the third one through the delivery door. Using the old building plans you obtained, we should be able to find the way to the controlled-access top-secret areas."

Hossein nodded in agreement. "We can then follow personnel into sensitive areas with the MAVs."

"You've got it." As groups of employees entered, Pat used the notebook to direct the MAVs inside the building. Each camera view appeared separately in spilt-screens on the computer monitor. They could see employees walking past security stations and down long corridors, and they listened to their conversations. The video images, audio sounds, and GPS coordinates were recorded for transmittal to the CIA, where the data will be analyzed and utilized for potential air strikes.

Pat held his breath as a man swatted at a MAV, believing it was merely a flying insect. "Damn it, Hossein! That's Andrei Desnov, the Russian SVR agent that tailed me in Istanbul a few days ago. I wonder what evil mischief he's up to. Maybe he's here to check the site's security precautions." Pat directed one of the MAVs to follow right behind Desnov.

"Pat, Russian and Iranian engineers recently tested the Bushehr nuclear reactor that Russia helped build. It is ready to start up now, and maybe that is why Desnov is here."

"Yes, the Russians made a great deal of money on that project. Did you know the spent fuel from Bushehr can be converted into plutonium for use in nuclear warheads?"

"No, I did not." An Iranian walking with Desnov peered into an iris scanner and inserted an ID card in a card reader. When the door opened, Pat guided a MAV into the top-secret area with them.

"That is Doctor Ali Kermani escorting Desnov. He is a major VEVAK field agent!" Hossein exclaimed.

Doctor Ali Kermani felt satisfied that his country's nuclear research facilities are secure. He receives daily telex reports in his Evin Prison office from each nuclear location, and the memos always indicate the facilities are progressing toward the primary goal of building nuclear warheads.

Like his nation's fervent religious leaders, Kermani harbors an intense craving to wipe Israel off the map. He knows the day is not far off when Iran's long-range missiles will be armed with coveted nuclear warheads. A plan will then be devised to eradicate Israel, and any other country that comes to the Zionist's aid. He can hardly wait for the onset of the *jihad*. He believes the world will realize on that day that Iran is a regional superpower and one of the most powerful nations in the world. That will signal the rebirth of the Persian Empire!

Kermani was a young soldier in the Iranian Army during the Shah's regime in the late 1970s. However, he unloaded his rifle, put flowers in the muzzle, and defected to the rebels when the Islamic Revolution broke out in February 1979.

Kermani joined radical militants when they stormed the U.S. Embassy in Tehran during November 1979 and subsequently took Americans hostage. He often bragged how he scared the U.S. Marine guards so much that they would not even pick up their weapons to protect their embassy. He worked for months sorting shredded U.S. papers, and successfully put together several top-secret documents.

Drafted back into the Iranian Army during the Iran-Iraq War, Kermani was chosen to be an intelligence officer. He earned a reputation as a relentless, sadistic interrogator of captured Iraqi soldiers, and expressed an intense hatred of the Arabs.

After the war, Kermani earned a Master of Science degree and then a doctorate at the University of Tehran. He was hired as a mid-level field agent in the Ministry of Intelligence and Security, Iran's Secret Police, VEVAK, shortly after receiving his Ph.D. The government paid for all of his college expenses and demanded that he sign a contract requiring eight years of service to the nation.

Now middle aged and balding, Kermani enjoys working out of his office at Evin. It is close to his villa in the northern Tehran Shemiran district, where he lives with his obedient *khanom* and three young children. However, more importantly, he has access to Evin Prison where he can continually hone his torture techniques on the inmates. He openly brags about his involvement with the rape, torture, and subsequent death of Iranian-Canadian photojournalist, Zahra Kazemi, in 2003. Kazemi had been arrested and then incarcerated in Evin Prison for taking photographs in front of the facility.

Narcissistic and an incredible egotist, Doctor Ali Kermani is proud to be the namesake of Mohammed's son-in-law, Ali, and he most certainly lets everyone know it. He does not realize that he is a miscreant.

★★★

"Now I know Desnov is up to no good," Pat stated. The display on his notebook showed the VEVAK and SVR agents walking past a natural uranium storage area in the Jabr Ibn Hayan Multipurpose Laboratories. "They converted UF4 into uranium metal there in 2000." The MAV picked up portions of conversations, indicating the Iranian and Russian agents were pleased with security precautions at the facility. They heard Kermani and Desnov mention inspecting the Isfahan Nuclear Technology and Research Center. Pat exclaimed loudly, "I pray to God that Zivah doesn't tangle with the two of them when they get to Isfahan!"

Pat directed another MAV to follow a scientist into the Molybdenum, Iodine, and Xenon Radioisotope Production Laboratory. Hossein translated the posted Persian signs and casual conversations, indicating the presence of nuclear materials. Pat said, "The International Atomic Energy Agency has been trying to verify that unreported nuclear material was imported to Iran back in 1991. It's too bad they didn't have MAVs for surveillance then. However, we *now* have recorded proof that the nuclear material does exist."

He directed a third MAV to follow another scientist into the Research Reactor Facility. Between Hossein's translations of the posted signs and the chatter of casual conversations, they determined the facility was producing small amounts of plutonium from spent nuclear fuel. "Aha," Pat remarked, "We have empirical evidence that this location is actively working toward creating nuclear warheads. That cinches it. We'd better take out this entire facility before the Russian Ministry of Atomic Energy fulfills its contract to provide Iran with Atomic Vapor Laser Isotope Separating equipment. That technology would give Iran the means to produce quantities of highly enriched uranium for nuclear weapons of mass destruction."

He recalled all three MAVs by directing them to follow employees exiting the complex. Pat uploaded the photos, recordings, and site coordinates to his BlackBerry and then transmitted them to Langley. He sent a text message to Langley and the team, "*delta one site confirmed soft and good to go. viper leader.*" While packing up the notebook and MAVs, he said, "Okay, we're out of here."

About then, Pat received a text message from Langley, "*viper leader. inspect echo site tomorrow. hq.*"

"Hossein, we'll check out the Parchin facility in the morning."

Day Four: Viper Leader

Pat and Hossein were up before dawn. Heading south, Hossein drove past the University of Tehran. It was still dark and the campus was deserted. Pat remarked, "I studied Islamic Philosophy and Mysticism here in the late 1970s. Those were sure violent days at the university, with frequent anti-Shah demonstrations and Islamic fanatics throwing acid in the faces of women not wearing *chadors*."

Merchants were setting up gold chains, Persian carpets, spices, and other displays as Hossein drove past the Grand Bazaar. "This is still the largest bazaar in the Middle East, Pat."

"Yes, and I recall roaming through the miles and miles of narrow streets in the bazaar. I'll also never forget the disgusting stench of the men's room there. I wouldn't even go in that pig sty."

"I agree with that!" Driving through southern Tehran, Hossein remarked, "This is the poorest area in the city. Some of the uneducated residents are afraid to use the purified tap water, perhaps because they are illiterate. They get their drinking and cooking water from ancient contaminated wells, or worse, from the dirty *jubes*."

"Yes, I've seen the residents washing dishes, brushing their teeth, and drinking the water in those deep gutters years ago," Pat agreed. "Many of the servants in affluent northern Tehran even washed their employer's household dishes in the *jubes*. Perhaps they thought the running mountain water was clean up there, but I wouldn't use it!"

To avoid a known Ansar-e-Hezbollah roadblock on the Tehran-Parchin Road, Hossein drove into the holy city of Rey. They went by the Mongol Tower built during the Genghis Khan invasion. Then they passed by the Islamic Shrine of *Imam* Hossein, a descendant of Ali Reza, the venerated eighth Shiite *Imam*, just as the call to prayer emitted from one of the minarets. Pilgrims were beginning to enter the shrine grounds, and Hossein stated, "The *Imams* are divinely inspired Shiite religious leaders."

"I understand they're also considered to be saints."

"That's right. The worshipers will enter the gold-domed mosque containing the tomb of *Imam* Hossein and touch the precious silver grille while praying to Allah."

They continued southeast, past the 600 A.D. Sassanian Fire Temple in Tappeh. Hossein offered, "The Zoroastrians worshiped here long before the Arab invasion and the subsequent conversion of the Persians to Islam."

"I studied the ancient Zoroastrian religion in college, and I believe the fire temples were their places of worship. They used clean, white ash from the fires during purification ceremonies."

"That is correct, Pat. They did not worship fire, but kept the temple fires burning constantly."

They continued up the road to Varamin. After passing by the Mongol tomb-tower of Ala'eddin, Hossein turned on the paved road heading northeast. Pat said, "That dirt track to the southeast is where I rode an ornery camel into the desert with a tourist caravan years ago. We went out to the Shah Abbas Caravansary in the Great Salt Desert, and our caravan followed the ancient Silk Road."

"We call it the *Dasht-e-Kavir* wilderness."

"Yes, I remember that from my last tour of duty here," Pat replied. "Just a few miles east is where eight American servicemen died in the parched desert during the aborted 'Operation Eagle Claw' mission in April 1980. They were attempting to free me and the other hostages held by Khomeini's goons."

After going through the tiny mud hut village of Evane Kay, Hossein drove over a bridge spanning the Damavand River. Nearing the desert town of Parchin, he warned, "We are getting close, Pat. Maybe we should hike up one of the hills here, before we're close enough to be spotted by the security forces."

"Good idea. We'll get our bearings, and then decide where to setup our MAV launch site." They pulled off the paved road, hid the Mercedes behind a small rise, and climbed a sand dune covered with low-growing desert plants. The duo spooked an Asian gazelle at the top of the dune. "This terrain reminds me of the Mojave Desert in Southern California."

"Look, Pat, we can see the secured site where we suspect they are developing and testing nuclear weapons. The Iranian government refused the International Atomic Energy Agency's request to inspect the site."

"Yep, it's a logical site for development of the high explosive components required for implosion-type nuclear weapons. Intel has evidence that chemical weapons are also developed at this vast complex. They also tell us that this site, as well as all other nuclear development sites in Iran, is protected by anti-aircraft missiles. You put the MAVs on that flat rock while I ready the notebook." Pat took telephotos of the facility, then launched several MAVs and directed them toward the site. Watching the split-screen images, he remarked, "That half-buried facility looks like the high explosive testing bunker identified in the Israeli fly-over camera photographs. We'll check it out." He directed a MAV to follow a scientist into the bunker.

After reading the Persian signs and listening to several casual technical discussions, Hossein declared, "This is a mock-up site for a nuclear explosion. They will use depleted uranium as a surrogate for the explosion, instead of highly enriched uranium."

"We definitely want to take out that research bunker!"

Pat then directed a pair of MAVs toward two igloo-shaped structures in the main area. "That looks like another hazardous testing facility. Let's go in for a look." Pat directed MAVs into each of the structures. While observing the interiors on split-screens, he said, "You know, Intel suggests these buildings may be involved in high explosive shrapnel tests. But, I don't see evidence of anything going on right now."

Pointing up the hill, Hossein exclaimed, "It looks like they are tunneling into the side of the hill about a kilometer above the igloos. Perhaps it is for armament testing."

"Or may be for underground nuclear weapons testing. Although, it's too close to the rest of the other facilities . . . and the town. Nonetheless, they may not care about what's in the immediate area when testing nukes. I don't understand how they would be that idiotic." He directed the MAVs out of the igloos and up the hill to the tunnel.

"It looks like they are tunneling at a downward slope, Pat."

"That's an indication they'll use the site for full-scale underground nuclear weapon tests. This cinches it . . . now we have the proof we need and I believe we should destroy the tunnel."

"Yes. Recently, a government deputy from Isfahan publicly announced there is a large underground nuclear research facility near the town of Parchin. I think we have found it."

"It would be a plus if we could also destroy the co-located chemical weapons facility." Pat recalled the MAVs. Then he uploaded the photos, recordings, and site GPS coordinates to his BlackBerry. He immediately transmitted them to Langley. "Hossein, we had better pack up and get out of here before we're spotted."

"Oh, Allah help us, Pat! Look at the dust trail heading in our direction. We are already spotted." Hossein tripped while going down the hill as he sidestepped to avoid a cobra, and the MAV case went flying out of his hands. Pat caught it in mid-air and they hustled toward the Mercedes.

After placing the surveillance gear in the trunk, Pat got behind the wheel and started the vehicle. A shot rang out and Hossein screamed, "I am hit in the shoulder!"

Pat readied his UZI as he jumped out of the Mercedes. However, he calmly placed the weapon on top of the car and raised his hands when he saw an Iranian holding a 9-millimeter ZOAF semi-auto pistol at Hossein's head. The man yelled in Persian, "I am Hassan Degani, VEVAK agent. Keep your hands up and walk toward me. Who are you and what are you doing here?"

Pat approached, and Degani started to lower his pistol from Hossein's head to point it at him. Then Pat swiftly kicked the man's left knee, breaking the joint and dropping him to the ground. Although crippled and screaming in pain, Degani reached for his fallen pistol a few feet away. As he grabbed it, Pat crushed his throat with a sharp karate chop to the Adam's apple. Degani did not utter another sound. He just fell over dead. Pat whispered, "My instructors at The Farm taught me that rules don't apply in this kind of mortal combat."

Wincing with pain from his gunshot wound, Hossein uttered, "You just killed the paramour of Doctor Ali Kermani. It is told that Kermani always took him on business trips because the young agent was a satisfactory substitute for his wife, as she could not travel with him. Moreover, Hassan translates to *Good,* and they say that Kermani thought Degani was very good at satisfying his abnormal sexual desires. He might be close by, so we should get out of here now."

As Pat put a bandage over Hossein's bleeding wound, he proffered, "I heard stories about that kind of shameless arrangement when I was stationed here. And Iran's president says there aren't homosexuals in *his* country?" Pat helped his friend into the Mercedes and he drove north toward the town of Damavand. Traveling at up to 150 miles per hour on the straight-aways in the turbo-powered vehicle, Pat easily out distanced any potential pursuers. Just south of Damavand, they skirted around the town on a gravel road and entered the paved Tehran-Damavand highway to the west about halfway to the capital.

Hossein looked pale from loss of blood when he told Pat, "I need medical treatment, and you must stop at my good friend's home, Doctor Majid Isfahani, on the eastside. He is anti-government and will help us. Although, he believes VEVAK has him under surveillance."

"Will do. Hang on, Hossein, and tell me how to get there."

"He lives in the Narmak district, just off the Damavand Highway. Take a right on Shahdari, then left on Aghaz and right on Eslami. His villa is on the left."

Pat found Doctor Isfahani's home and rushed Hossein inside. As the doctor patched up his friend, Pat sent Langley and the team a text message, "*echo site confirmed soft and good to go. contact wounded. viper leader.*"

Langley replied, "*viper leader. get out of there asap. hq.*"

Doctor Isfahani advised, "The bullet went clean through without hitting a bone. He is weak, but not critical, and I can care for him here. However, it may be a few days before he can travel."

"That's great, Doctor, because there would be too many questions asked at a hospital. Hossein has done more than his share for our mission, so keep him down as long as you can." Pat then drove toward Hossein's villa on the north side of town.

Day Five: Viper Leader

The phone rang at six in the morning and woke Pat out of a restless sleep. Azar pounded on the bedroom door and screamed, "They arrested my husband!"

Pat ran into the next room and picked up the phone. Doctor Isfahani anxiously exclaimed, "VEVAK agents came to my villa while I was at the office getting pain medication for Hossein. My servants said they are taking him to Evin Prison for questioning. He will never leave that wicked place alive."

"I'm just a few minutes away from Evin. Maybe I can beat them there."

"Good. Allah be with you. They are looking for me now, so I will drive to the Turkish border before they find and arrest me."

"*Khoob, merci maemnum. Khoda Hafez*, good doctor." Pat immediately left for Evin. It was an overcast morning as he parked the Mercedes across the street from the prison's main entrance five minutes later and prepared for a firefight. Full of adrenalin and anticipation, thoughts ran rampant through his head, *The extra 40-round magazines will be a Godsend. If I run out of ammo, or if the UZI jams, I'll have to use my Glock. Maybe I should use the pistol first, with the silencer attached . . . that way I won't attract as much attention. What if the guards come pouring out of the prison?*

Pat's thoughts were interrupted by the sound of two vehicles coming down the parkway at high speed. He immediately went into Condition Black, the combat mode, and his reflexes and instincts took over. Crouching behind the Mercedes, with the UZI steadied on the hood, he shot out the right front tire of the first vehicle with a 3 to 4 round full-automatic burst. The driver lost control of his vehicle, jumped the sidewalk, and hit a concrete utility pole head-on. Either stunned or dead, no one exited the automobile.

The second vehicle glanced off the rear bumper of the first car and that driver brought his car to a screeching halt in the middle of the street. Three men jumped out of the vehicle, one of them dragging Hossein along with him, and headed for the prison entrance. All three were shooting in Pat's direction with semi-auto pistols. Pat easily took out the first two with automatic fire from the UZI, hitting them with multiple 9-millimeter bullets in their chests and throats. It was not safe to use the submachine gun on the third agent holding on to Hossein. Moreover, the man was wearing a bulletproof vest. Pat quickly dropped the UZI and drew the Glock from his holster. With a two-hand hold, he put the red laser sight dot on the forehead of the man, followed him as he ran, held his breath, and squeezed the trigger. Andrei Desnov, Russian SVR agent, went down forever with one well-placed 9-millimeter bullet in his forehead.

Handcuffed, and in pain from his gunshot wound, Hossein stumbled across the parkway. Pat ran up to him, helped him into the Mercedes, and immediately sped off toward the north. Evin Prison guards poured out onto the parkway and fired at the vehicle with Khaybar assault rifles. "Keep your head down, Hossein!" Pat yelled as several 5.56-millimeter bullets blew out the rear window. They rounded a curve and were soon out of the line of fire.

Hossein moaned and whispered weakly, "Pat, do not lead them to my villa. You have to head for Shemshak in the Alborz Mountains."

"I know the way, I've been there before. Just keep an eye out for pursuers." He left the city and drove up into the barren mountains on Shemshak Road. Pat stopped momentarily and took the handcuffs off his friend. To get Hossein's mind off his painful wound, he said, "Look. There's the Assassins Castle on top of that rugged peak with the steep cliffs. That's a weird coincidence, since I just assassinated a major Russian agent!"

Continuing higher up the road, Pat pulled into the Shemshak Lodge parking lot and backed into a spot to hide the shot-out rear window. He looked around for security guards watching over the guests' vehicles. Seeing none, he ordered, "Let's go, Hossein! We have to steal a car because they'll be looking for the Mercedes." Pat hotwired a nondescript tan-colored Pakan and they took off, heading deeper into the mountains. "Do you remember that narrow road that goes down the steep grade to the Chalus-Karaj Highway just north of Karaj Lake?"

"Yes, they will never believe we would escape using that route!"

"You're right. They also won't believe we would head back to Tehran via the Karaj Highway. We'll pick up your wife and you can get her safely into Turkey before the fireworks start. Let's go for it." Pat went west, passing by the Dizin Ski Resort. He then headed down the treacherous grade. "I was in a white-out blizzard the last time I drove this road, Hossein. Believe it or not, an *Irani* heading up the mountain toward me stopped to say my headlights were on!"

"I believe it. Persians have always been lousy drivers, and most of them seem to lack common sense while driving."

At the bottom of the grade, they stopped at a teahouse on the Chalus-Karaj Highway next to the Karaj River. Pat checked Hossein's bandages for signs of bleeding from his gunshot wound, but he appeared to be okay. Using five-rial coins, Hossein called his home from an outdoor payphone. "Azar, listen very carefully. I escaped and VEVAK is after us! You must pack your gold jewelry, our important papers, bandages, and all our money. Do it right now . . . we'll pick you up soon. Do not call your parents. We will contact them when we are safely out of Persia." He hung up before Azar could object or question him.

The two continued into Tehran under cover of darkness. Pat bypassed the area around Evin Prison, which was a hotbed of police activity. Taking *kuches* and other small side streets, he managed to avoid multiple checkpoints while heading toward the Taj Rish district.

Covered head to toe in her black *chador*, Azar was anxiously waiting in the shadows of her villa's entrance with two small suitcases and a large handbag. Pat tossed the luggage into the trunk of the Pakan, helped Hossein into the rear seat with Azar, and sped off. Azar changed her husband's bandages and determined his wound wasn't infected or bleeding. Pat and Hossein then excitedly explained what had transpired during their long day as they headed west out of town.

"It's not safe for us to stay in Tehran, so we'll drive to Alev's cousin's home in Tabriz. I can coordinate the mission from there. Azar will have to drive the Pakan the rest of the way to the border at Razi. I'll make arrangements for CIA and OHD agents to meet you at Kapikoy on the Turkish side and escort you safely to Ankara."

"Excellent," Hossein replied. "Maybe we can obtain political asylum in the United States. Then we can live near my sister in California."

"I'll work on that possibility," Pat promised.

After passing through the towns of Karaj, Abyek, and Sharifabad, Pat headed southwest into the desert on a dirt track. "I know where there's an archeological dig in the middle of nowhere, and it should be a safe place to get some sleep. The professor of my Archeology of Iran class at the University of Tehran conducted a field trip there once." He pulled in behind a sand dune next to the dig site, and then climbed up it to see if anyone was nearby. Satisfied they were alone, Pat offered, "I'll take the first watch and wake you in an hour or two, Hossein."

Azar exclaimed, "This place looks familiar . . . I believe my university class worked on the dig here too. I can also stand watch."

The two men nodded in agreement and Hossein said, "You can take the second watch, Dear. I need the sleep."

Day Six: Viper Leader

They were up at dawn. Using a Sterno can, Azar quickly prepared hot *chahee* to go with the *nan-e-bahr-bahr-ee* and goat cheese she cleverly remembered to bring. They were soon on a dirt track heading west. Pat remarked, "We'll stay on desert tracks until we reach Takestan village. That'll keep us out of Qazvin, where I know roadblocks will be looking for us."

"I am sure they will. We may have to skirt around Zandjan as well," Hossein replied.

Back on the paved highway, Pat continued driving west. They went through Shanat and Soltaniyeh villages. As a precaution, they dropped down into the Zandjan-chay River *wadi* a few miles east of the town of Zandjan. He drove slowly alongside the dry riverbed to prevent creating a dust trail that could be seen from the town and attract attention to them. Several miles west of Zandjan, he pulled back up on the highway and sped off toward Tabriz.

Traveling at high speeds, Pat only slowed down while going through the town of Miyaneh and the villages of Qarachaman and Bostanabad. They were at Nader's villa by mid-day.

Pat told Hossein and Azar how he and Alev entered Iran several days earlier and suggested they take the same route in reverse. Then he said, "Hide the stolen Pakan just outside Razi and walk to the border crossing. Our agents will be waiting for you on the Turkey side. He handed Hossein an envelope containing $5,000 U.S. and continued, "Good luck and farewell, my dear friends." Pat saluted Hossein and declared, "You certainly displayed courage while under fire. Go with God!"

As Hossein and Azar left, Nader came out of his villa and greeted Pat with a warm, "Welcome back to my home. Alev and Ari are here."

Pat responded with, "I know. I also need refuge." He then sent a text message to Langley and the rest of the team, "*viper leader safe at location charlie.*"

Inside the villa, Pat greeted Gesoo. Then Alev ran over to him and, with a big smile, gave him a long, long hug. She kissed him on both cheeks and uttered, "I really missed you, Patrick. Let me tell you all about the events of the last two days." But first, she contemplated, *Eat your heart out Zivah, I'm back with Patrick now!*

Then Ari greeted Pat and said, "I'm ready to get out of Persia!"

With a wide grin, Pat declared, "Good. We leave in the morning." While shaking Ari's hand, he continued, "They may be looking for us at the Razi-Kapikoy crossing, so we'll cross at Sero-Esendere." Pat dreamt about Zivah all that night.

CHAPTER FOUR: CHALUS

Like many Iranian women, Hamideh is very attractive. She has a smooth, dark complexion, long straight black hair, haunting coal-black eyes, and the typical prominent Persian nose. The thirty-five-year-old lives with her parents, Hesam and Asal, on the family tea plantation near the Caspian Sea. Her father has roots in the region's Azeri tribe, and her mother is a Turkoman from near the Turkmenistan border in northeast Iran.

Hesam is an accomplished *setar* player, and he taught Hamideh how to play the four-string Persian musical instrument at a very young age. She loves playing the *setar*, which originated in Persia centuries ago. However, under the present Iranian regime, she is forbidden to play a musical instrument in public, as are all women in Iran.

She earned a Bachelor of Science degree in Agriculture at the College of Agriculture and Natural Resources, University of Tehran. After graduation, Hamideh worked on the family plantation and used her college education to help improve the family crops.

Hamideh was a mere child when the Ayatollah Khomeini Islamic Revolution changed the face of Iran in 1979, and she does not know much about that era. However, she hated the cultural changes that occurred as she matured, essentially because of the increasing horrendous restrictions placed on females in her nation.

She secretly converted from Islam to Christianity while in college, joining about 30,000 other Muslims in Iran that also converted over the years. Hamideh knew perfectly well that she would be killed instantly if Islamic radicals discover her secret conversion, because the nation's leaders follow strict Shariah law. This Islamic law decrees that converts from Islam to other religions must be sentenced to death.

Hamideh is upset about the occasional beheading over minor traffic accidents, and many other atrocious acts of violence by her countrymen. She is also concerned about a ban on the teaching of music in state and private schools, because the ruling *mullahs* claim that using musical instruments is contrary to the principles of the nation's Islamic value system.

Hamideh is ready and willing to help anyone who can change the existing conditions and perhaps even overthrow the oppressive clergy-controlled government. Therefore, when an old college roommate, also a Christian convert, contacted her about getting involved in a clandestine multinational spy mission in Iran, she eagerly volunteered to help. Moreover, she is anxious for some excitement in her mundane life.

Day Three continued: Copperhead

Alev and Hamideh enjoyed a scrumptious breakfast of *kaku sabzi*, the famous Persian caviar and egg frittata. Asal served it with fresh-picked white mulberries and hot Caspian *chahee*.

The duo put on black *chadors*, and then Hamideh drove her 1970s vintage Chevy Blazer down the palm tree lined streets of Chalus. While passing by the Enghelab Khazar Hotel on the shore of the Caspian Sea, she turned to Alev and commented, "That was the Caspian Hyatt Regency Hotel before the Islamic revolution. It was a popular place for foreigners working in Tehran to go and relax during the Shah's regime. They had a casino with gaming tables and slot machines, a cocktail lounge, and an excellent continental-style restaurant. Now, of course, gambling and drinking alcoholic beverages are against our Islamic law so the casino and cocktail lounge are gone."

Alev replied, with obvious resentment over Pat's rebuff of her advances and apparent jealousy of his relationship with Zivah, "I remember Patrick talking about staying there while he was stationed at the American Embassy in Tehran." She sarcastically continued, "They probably had Turkish belly dancers for entertainment!"

"They may have. I was just a toddler then. It sounds like you have a soft spot in your heart for Patrick."

"I believe I do. If only he would give me a chance to find out for sure. However, I would love to sleep with him, just for the thrill of the experience."

With a smile, Hamideh nodded in acknowledgement and then continued, "The Enghelab Khazar still has a top-class restaurant and it offers unimaginable luxury for a hotel in Iran."

Driving along the beach road, Alev asked, "What are all those birds over there?"

"Well, I see a lot of seagulls and a group of Caspian terns." Pointing toward the sea, she continued, "Look at the Caspian seal basking in the sun on the water's edge!"

"Are they all that small?"

"Yes, our seals are very small and they have light colored spots on their backs."

"Just like the seal pups in Turkish waters. This region reminds me of the Anatolian shoreline on the Aegean Sea. I love that part of my country."

By prior arrangement, the operatives met a Turkoman mountain guide, Saparmurat, at a teahouse near the Chalus Bazaar. The self-educated old man sported a brightly colored felt headdress. He was short and thin, and had a leathery face from being in the elements over the years. His slanted eyes, high cheekbones, yellowish skin tone, and other Mongolian-type features were typical of a Central Asian. Saparmurat had hunted in the wet and lush mountains overlooking the Caspian Sea during his adolescent years and all of his adult life. He certainly knew the region very well.

With a solemn look on his face, the man bowed as he greeted the two women. So he would not be overheard, he whispered in Persian, "I hate the ruling *mullahs* in Tehran. They think they are the only ones who know anything about Islamic theology. Now, what can I do for your cause?"

Alev sized him up, *He seems sincere and I think I can trust him. I just hope I'm right.*

Speaking softly, the two women stated their objective. He agreed to guide them to a position near the Chalus Nuclear Weapons Research site in the Alborz Mountains high above the Caspian Sea. "But, not too close because of the high security there," he cautioned.

Alev and Hamideh whispered in unison, "*Merci maemnum, Aga.*"

"Come with us," Alev offered, "and you will be paid well." Saparmurat picked up a rifle near the door as the trio left the teahouse. After heading south down the Chalus-Karaj Highway for several miles, Hamideh left the pavement and drove through the Caspian tea fields west of her home. She then used the Blazer's 4-wheel-drive feature to travel along narrow tracks high into the northern slopes of the Alborz Mountains.

Hamideh stopped under a tree when they reached the top of the timberline. Saparmurat said, "We must travel on foot from here. Follow me."

Alev and Hamideh removed their *chadors* and tossed them into the vehicle. Alev explained, "The black veils would stand out against the grayish-white granite in the mountains, and we could be spotted by security forces."

Saparmurat smiled as he admired their curvy figures clothed in western jeans and tight blouses as he thought, *I only see feminine shapes while inside my own home . . . just my family, never strangers. At least not since before the revolution when the Shah's government allowed men to sunbathe with women on the Caspian beaches.*

He led the way, carrying his old British Lee Enfield .303-caliber bolt-action carbine with a beat-up wood stock and rust spots on the barrel's exterior surface. The guide cautioned, "Watch out for cobras."

It was a steep, strenuous climb up and across an exposed granite ridge. Alev and Hamideh perspired from the heat and humidity, and they struggled with the weight of their surveillance gear, Alev's UZI with its extra 40-round magazines, and Hamideh's sawed-off double-barrel twelve gauge Hola shotgun. Then they dropped down into a high verdant valley. Saparmurat again cautioned the women, "Now you must look out for wild boar, wolves, jackals, and cheetahs . . . as well as cobras."

Just west of the mountain village of Marzanabad, after hiking about five miles across the mountains, Saparmurat led them up to a ridgeline very near the Kalar Dasht Plain. He told the two women to stay low. Then he pointed at the base of Mount Alam about a mile across the plain and stated, "That is what you are looking for. My job is done, if you can find your way back to the Blazer. I will walk back to town."

Alev handed the guide 40,000 *toman*, equivalent to about $39 U.S., and said, "*Merci maemnum, Aga. Khoda Hafez.*"

Saparmurat counted the 400,000 *rials*, and then grinned broadly while tossing his head to one side as a gesture of acceptance and appreciation. His parting words were, "Recent earthquakes caused numerous rockslides in this region, so be careful. With all those intense tremors, I would not want to be inside *that* mountain! *Khoda Hafez,* my friends."

With her high-powered binoculars, Alev observed hectic activity and intense security in front of the entrance to the underground nuclear weapons site tunneled into the mountain. "Hamideh, it's not safe to get closer. Get two Micro Aerial Vehicles ready to launch. I just hope the batteries hold up after traveling all that distance to the site and then returning back here." Hamideh set them up while Alev turned on the notebook computer. Alev took telephoto shots of the facility entrance. She then launched and directed the MAVs toward the research site.

Once the MAVs were inside the site, the operatives determined there were Russian, Red Chinese, North Korean, and Iranian scientists and technicians working on nuclear weapons development in the facility. Watching the split-screen displays on the notebook, Hamideh exclaimed, "The different groups of foreigners appear to have their own specialty tasks to perform. Did you know that the local citizens were told this is an electricity generation plant run by the Canadians? Of course, the Islamic government lied to us, as they usually do."

"I believe it. We both know that the incumbent Iranian leaders in Tehran are masters of deception!" Alev directed the MAVs toward several signs written in Persian. "Hamideh, my written Persian is not that great, as I have a little trouble reading it from right to left. Will you translate for me?"

Hamideh translated the signs, "This one says 'RADIATION. OBSERVE YOUR DOSIMETERS.' That one says 'WARHEAD AREA. KEEP OUT'. And, the sign on that door says 'RESTRICTED AREA. TOP SECRET CLEARANCE ONLY.'"

Alev directed one MAV to follow a scientist into the top-secret room. They observed atomic weapons design blueprints and cut-away models of delivery rockets equipped with nuclear warheads. "Hamideh, I also need your help with understanding some of the local dialect conversations."

"Those men appear to be from the Democratic People's Republic of Korea. However, they are talking in Persian about designing plutonium warheads. That other group is discussing rocket delivery systems that could reach Tel Aviv and Ankara."

"Just as I suspected. The dirty camels!" exclaimed Alev, "Iran recently tested a ballistic missile capable of striking Tel Aviv and Ankara, and perhaps even as far as central Europe."

Hamideh replied, "Our hard-line president is just rattling his saber and thumbing his nose at Israel, Turkey, all of Europe, and most of all, America. He said on television the other day that Iran now has a new unmanned bomber that can carry four cruise missiles, and it has a 620-mile range."

"Do you realize that Maku, in Northwest Iran, is only 600 miles from Ankara?"

Hamideh shook her head in disbelief and quietly said, "No, I did not, my friend."

Alev uploaded the photos, recordings, and site coordinates to her BlackBerry and transmitted them to Langley. Then she declared, "It's much more than saber rattling, dear Hamideh! And my country's survival is at stake." Alev recalled the MAVs and said, "You pack them up while I stow the notebook. Then we'd better get out of here before we're seen." She immediately sent Langley and the team a text message, "*foxtrot one site confirmed hardened and good to go. copperhead.*"

Langley replied, "*copperhead. get out of there asap. hq.*"

Crossing the last valley on the way back to the Blazer, they spotted a cheetah chasing an adolescent wild pig directly in front of them. Hamideh took the safety off her loaded shotgun and whispered, "Stop and don't move!" The two women froze until the animals were out of sight in the green foliage. "Cheetahs are so fast, that young boar will not have a chance of getting away from it."

"I believe it. Let's hurry up and get out of the mountains before dark." A cloudburst soaked them to the skin on the way down the slope. Back at their vehicle, Alev yelled, "I hate this wretched thing!" as she donned her black *chador* over her sopping-wet clothing.

"So do I, my good friend, so do I. The day will come when women in Persia will no longer have to abide by the strict, archaic *hijab* dress code. Then we can burn our *chadors*, just as the women's liberation movement in America burned their brassieres years ago. I certainly look forward to that momentous day, although it will probably take another revolution first."

Hamideh drove down the mountain and through the tea fields. They crossed the Chalus-Karaj Highway and onto the relative safety of her plantation. She parked the Blazer out of sight under a carport behind the farmhouse.

Day Four continued: Copperhead

Early the next morning, Alev was startled out of a deep sleep by the sound of a helicopter circling low overhead. She quickly woke the others and they all peered outside through the lace curtains. Hamideh exclaimed, "It is a Russian-made Mil Mi-8 gunship, and they are looking for someone or something. It might be us or maybe the Blazer if they spotted us in the mountains yesterday. They are the Army of the Guardians, and they have absolutely no qualms about using their weapons of war on Iranian citizens!"

"Hesam, Asal, Hamideh, get dressed and grab your valuables and guns. We must leave right now," Alev said excitedly. Waving them out of the house, she screamed, "Hurry up and get into my Samand! We'll flee through the apple orchard and try to elude them. We can't take a chance with the Blazer because they may have its description."

Alev drove into the orchard as soon as Hamideh and her parents were in the car. The helicopter crew spotted the vehicle speeding through the trees and fired one of their four missiles at them. Luckily, the missile missed them and hit a tree just as they went past it. Flying apples pelted the car. She immediately drove down into a riparian creek gully hidden from the air by overhanging cottonwood trees. Alev yelled, "Stay in the car!" as she grabbed her UZI and several extra magazines.

Hamideh yelled back, "We will," and cradled the sawed-off shotgun in her lap.

Alev ran out of the depression and into the orchard toward the blasted apple tree. Concealed in the shade of a tree, she readied her weapon for the next flyover of the circling helicopter. As it flew directly overhead at treetop level, she stepped out into the open, aimed the UZI at the helicopter's undercarriage, and emptied her 40-round magazine with full-automatic fire. She immediately employed a tactical reload and put another full magazine into the submachine gun. However, she did not need to use it because every 9-millimeter round had hit the target, thanks to her intensive training and expertise with the UZI. The helicopter burst into flames, went into a spin, crashed, and exploded a mere 100 feet from Alev as she stepped behind an apple tree for protection. She ran for the Samand

and hollered as she approached the creek, "I took out those dirty camels. Let's go!"

They sped through the orchard and out onto the Caspian Highway. Heading west toward Astara, Alev apologized, "Hamideh, I'm very sorry your parents had to get involved in our operation. I'll make sure you get safely across the Azerbaijan border."

"I would have moved them before the fireworks started anyway, because our home is just too close to the target. They knew how dangerous the mission would be and what to expect. So, we planned to relocate to Armenia where I can openly practice my Christian faith. We can always return to our homeland after the next revolution."

"It'll be good for you to get away from the religious, political, and gender repression in Iran. Keep an eye out for more helicopters and anyone who might be chasing us on the highway. I'll focus on what's ahead of us."

"Okay." Hamideh checked her shotgun and turned sideways to look out the rear window. With a solemn look at his daughter, Hesam nodded and patted an ancient .455-caliber break-top Webley revolver in his waistband. Asal had a tight grip on the family's cherished *setar*. "I know a vodka and caviar smuggler at Astara who will help us." Hamideh blushed and continued, "Firouz and I were, ah, very close friends in college. I never told my parents before, but he saved me from having acid tossed in my face at the university."

"Why would anyone do that to you?"

"I decided to not wear my *chador* or cover my hair one day and the campus radicals did not like it. Thank God, Firouz stopped them. I never tried that again! Such is life in oppressive Iran."

Alev remembered the Ansar-e-Hezbollah roadblock at Rasht when she and Pat were inserted a few days earlier.

With Hamideh's helpful knowledge of the area, she easily skirted around the town and avoided the possibility of another checkpoint.

"Maybe news about the helicopter you destroyed has not yet reached Rasht," Hamideh stated. Throwing her hands up, she continued, "Or, perhaps the Guardians' headquarters still does not know about the incident."

With apparent skepticism, Alev replied, "I sure hope you're right about that!"

They arrived at Astara nearly four hours after leaving Chalus, full of anxiety and fear of being killed or caught. "Turn right on this first street coming up and go down to the waterfront docks." Hamideh then directed Alev to her friend's motorized fishing boat. The smuggler was repairing fishing nets on the pier. Hamideh ran up to him, gave him a hug, kissed him on both cheeks, and stated, "We need your help, Firouz." She introduced her parents and Alev, and then explained their dire situation.

Firouz graciously welcomed them with a sincere smile and said, "Hamideh, you and your parents get on the vessel and stay out of sight below. Please help yourselves to the food and water. We will leave for Azerbaijan after nightfall."

Alev said farewell to her friends. Then, with a grateful smile, she handed Hamideh an envelope containing $5,000 U.S. and said, "Make a good life for your family in Armenia, dear friend. You did an excellent job for our cause and you are very courageous." Looking at Firouz, she continued, "You, Sir, take good care of them!"

"Do not worry. My vessel is powerful and very fast. No one can catch me, and I have contacts in the Republic of Azerbaijan town of Astara that will help them get to Armenia." He then told Alev how to avoid the checkpoint in town.

Alev bypassed the checkpoint, found the Astara-Tabriz Highway on the outskirts of the city, and headed west toward Tabriz and her cousin's home at high speed. However, a military vehicle pulled alongside of her Samand a few miles out of town. Although she was wearing a black *chador* that just showed her face, the soldier in the front passenger seat eyed her for a few moments, and then motioned for her to pull over and stop. She immediately pulled off the road and parked in the shade of a bridge crossing a small stream. Wild thoughts raced through her mind, *I don't know how they ever found me! I'll have to take them out. What if someone hears the gunfire? What if they have backup on the way?*

She decided the UZI would make too much noise when fired and could attract the attention of the locals, and perhaps carry all the way back to Astara. Alev drew the silencer-equipped 9-millimeter Zigana pistol from her cross-draw hip holster while getting out of the vehicle. She kept the weapon hid under her *chador* as two *Hezbollahis* approached with AK-47 assault weapons at the ready position and their fingers on the triggers. One of them commanded in *Farsi*, "Show me your identity papers, right now! We are checking all strangers in the area."

Alev murmured demurely to catch them off-guard, "*Baleh, Aga.*" She then pulled her pistol from beneath her veil, presented it with a two-hand hold, and deftly placed two rounds to the center of both of their chests. She followed-up with one round into each of their foreheads as she bitterly screamed, "More dirty camels bite the dust!" She dragged the two bodies under the bridge, and then moved their vehicle alongside them so it could not be seen from the highway.

Back on the road, Alev constantly scanned ahead, behind, and every conceivable hiding place along the way where more "dirty camels" might be lurking. The 175-mile trip from Astara took about four hours and the operative was nearly a near nervous wreck by the time she reached Tabriz.

Cousin Nader welcomed her at the gate of his villa. With her hands trembling, Alev said breathlessly, "I need refuge."

"Of course. You are always welcome here, My Dear Alev," he responded.

Inside the safety of Nader's home, Alev quickly tossed off her *chador* and greeted Nader's wife, Gesoo, with a heartfelt hug. Then she sent Langley and the team a text message, "*copperhead safe at location charlie.*"

CHAPTER FIVE: ARAK

Sadar is a dark-skinned Kurd freedom fighter in his late twenties with shiny black hair and coal-black eyes. He strongly desires the creation of an independent Kurdistan nation and believes the ideal location for the new territory would be in the mountainous area at the junction of the Turkey, Iran, and Iraq borders. This is the historic region of Kurdistan, a nation without a country. Sadar is a proud member of the government resistance organization, the Democratic Party of Iranian Kurdistan.

A descendant of the ancient Medes in Persia, Sadar dresses in the typical Kurdish style; billowing pantaloons with pegged ankles, a loose fitting military-type tunic tucked into his pants, narrow and colorful cummerbund, and a dark silky turban. A large, shiny-bladed Kurdish knife with a decorative hilt is stuck into his cummerbund. His lineage can be traced back to Saladin, the noted Sunni Muslim adversary of the Crusaders during the 12th century.

Although Kurds are largely Sunni, Sadar and his family are part of a very small minority that practice Judaism. Like most of the Kurd mountain people, he is not well educated. Nevertheless, he is extremely intelligent and astute, and he certainly would have excelled if given the opportunity to attend college. He and his parents live in a small mountain village, and his sister lives in Sanandaj with her Kurdish husband. Sadar did have several Kurdish female friends over the years, but none that he seriously considered marrying.

Sadar was merely ten years old during the Kurdish uprising in Iraq in 1991. However, he vividly remembers the suppression of his people and the brutal recapture of the Kurdish areas by Saddam Hussein's troops. That is when

80

his family packed their belongings and migrated across the border to the Zagros Mountains in Iran. Today, however, Iranian government sources claim that the Kurds' desire for autonomy is the most serious internal problem facing the nation. Life is not going too well for Sadar and his family because the fervent radical *mullahs* ruling Iran are so anti-Kurd, as well as anti-Sunni and anti-Jew. Thus, he did not hesitate to volunteer to help the coalition of CIA, OHD, Mossad, and MI6 operatives during their covert mission in Iran.

Day Two continued: Asp

Ari and Sadar were up early and enjoyed a light breakfast of warm and tasty *nan-e-bahr-bahr-ee*, tangy goat cheese, and hot coffee. While eating, Ari asked Sadar, "Would you like to stop at the tombs of Esther and Mordecai on the way out of town?"

"Of course I would. You probably know my family converted to Judaism when they migrated to Iran in 1991. I felt very humble and religious at the shrine the last time I was there."

Ari's great-uncle, Abraham, interjected, "It is cared for by the Islamic Revolutionary authorities now. So be careful!"

"We will," replied Ari, "See you tonight, Uncle Abraham, Yahweh willing."

"Good, Ari. You know how proud I am to be named after my Old Testament ancestor, the Prophet Abraham, which translates to Father of a Mighty Nation."

"I certainly do."

Sadar drove the Land Rover down Engelab Boulevard and went past the Baba Taher Tomb. "That is the burial place of the famous Sufi poet. Baba Taher was the grandson of Omar Khayyam." Ari nodded in acknowledgement.

Sadar then parked near the Mausoleum of Esther and Mordecai. The two men climbed the outdoor stairs to the first floor roof where they were given skullcaps to don before entering the shrine room. A Muslim docent explained, "Queen Esther was the beautiful Jewish wife of Persia's King Xerxes. She immigrated to Persia with her uncle, Mordecai, to try to obtain the king's protection for all the Jews living in the Persian Empire. Of course, she was successful and married the king when he fell in love with her." Ari and Sadar just smiled and did not acknowledge that they knew the Old Testament Book of Esther story extremely well. The two operatives recited their Hebrew prayers in silence.

After leaving the holy shrine, Sadar drove past the Ibn Sina Memorial. "Ibn Sina, known as Avecina in the West, was one of the most influential Persian scholars in the world."

"Yes. I studied his ideas and observations on logic, philosophy, science, and metaphysics while attending college," Ari replied. "He was also a great 11th century medical doctor, and I read the Hebrew translation of his *Cannon of Medicine* masterpiece. Avecina's discussion on scorpions and the treatment of their stings ten centuries ago is still relevant information today."

They headed southeast out of the city and then turned due east at the town of Malayer. The locals eyed the Land Rover with suspicion, or perhaps just curiosity, as they went through the small village of Amirabad. When Sadar reached the town of Khondab, he turned southeast again and cautioned, "We are getting close to the nuclear site. We must watch for security patrols now."

"We're about 35 miles north of the city of Arak now. According to my GPS, this small paved road we're

82

approaching goes directly to the Arak Heavy-water Nuclear Reactor site just east of here."

"I believe you are right, Ari. But we cannot drive up there without being spotted. How do we get closer to the facility?"

"We'll just have to wait until nightfall, and then we can hike in under the cover of darkness. I'm glad Uncle Abraham gave us plenty of food and water when we left his villa this morning. Meanwhile, we may as well drive into the city, because we may raise suspicions if we stay around here the rest of the day."

"Okay, you are the boss." Sadar continued down the highway toward Arak. There was an unexpected Iranian Revolutionary Guard Corps checkpoint in the village of Javarseyan. "Oh no, we are in big trouble now!"

"Sadar! Just stay calm. We'll tell them we are gold merchants and we have business to conduct at the Arak Bazaar."

The armed checkpoint leader held his left hand up and they came to a complete stop. He demanded in *Farsi*, "Give me your papers please. What is your business here?"

As he reviewed their documents, Sadar explained, "We are gold merchants from Hamadan, and we have business to conduct at the Arak Bazaar."

"Why are you on this side road instead of the main highway?"

Ari interjected, "We are sorry, *Aga*, but we had plenty of time to drive through the countryside and enjoy the natural beauty of the area," as he handed the leader 50,000 *toman* rolled up in the palm of his hand for *bakeesh*.

The Revolutionary Guard took his finger off the trigger of his KH-2002 carbine to accept the bribe. Then, with a wide grin, he ordered, "Get on your way and do not return to Hamadan on this road. Use the main highway!"

Ari and Sadar both said "*Merci maemnum, Aga. Khoda Hafez.*"

"*Khoda Hafez*, merchants," was the now *almost* friendly response.

Sadar proceeded on and then turned east on the main highway to the city. They drove through the village of Senejan and then went past several aluminum and petro-chemical plants just before entering Arak. "Did you know that Russian Intelligence believes some of these civilian plants may be fronts for the development of unguided rockets and SCUD missiles?"

"No, I did not know that, Ari. But, I do know that Arak is one of the main industrial cities in the nation." Entering the town, Sadar continued, "Quite a few Lurs live here. They are a tribe within the Kurdish nation."

"Yes, during my mission orientation, I was told the Lur nomads are actually a division of the ancient Kurds."

The desert city was surrounded by arid, brownish mountains to the east, south, and west. Sadar drove past the Azad University of Arak and down Fadaeiyan-e-Eslam Street. He parked on a side street near the Arak Bazaar. "I know a quiet restaurant around the corner where we can enjoy some excellent *chelo kebab*. The proprietor is a Lur, and he will keep quiet about our visit."

"Sounds good to me! I'm starved."

Walking into the Aga Khan Restaurant, Sadar hailed the owner, "Vafa, *Salaam! Hale shoma chetowre?*"

Vafa responded, "*Shalom,* my good friend. I am good. How are your parents?"

"They are doing well, thank you. This is my friend Ari, and we wish to enjoy some of your delicious *chelo kebab*."

As the two operatives finished their meal of rice and lamb kebabs, dozens of shouting demonstrators ran past the restaurant. Local policemen in riot gear followed close on their heels. "It sounds like there are dozens of people chanting from the rooftops," Ari said. Several rifle shots rang out and he exclaimed, "Those are not rubber bullets, those are real bullets because I can hear the 'crack' when they break the sound barrier!"

Vafa immediately locked his front door and explained, "They are demonstrating against the recent presidential election results. Many people believe fraud was involved and the popular runner-up should have won. They are chanting in support of him."

Sadar added, "No one believes the incumbent president won the election!"

Vafa continued, "Hurry, my friends, leave by the back door and go down the *kuche* to your machine before they set it on fire to ward off the effects of tear gas."

"I remember that this is how the Ayatollah Ruhollah Khomeini Islamic Revolution started in 1978," Ari stated, "I wonder if it will happen again?"

"I do not know. However, Iran's Supreme Leader warned the reformist opposition groups that they will face harsh responses from the government, and I believe it."

Sadar and Ari rushed out of town and avoided more riots in the streets. They headed west on the main highway and turned north toward Javarseyan. "I am glad we are out of the city. I sense big trouble brewing for the Iranian government soon."

"You're right, Sadar. This may be the beginning of the end of the current Iranian hard-line regime. Right now, we must find a detour around the Revolutionary Guard roadblock at Javarseyan."

About three miles south of the village, Sadar spotted a dirt road heading across the desert toward the hills to the west. "This track may take us around the town."

"Good. Just take your time, Sadar, and it will be dusk by the time we get to the nuclear site."

Sadar drove very slowly to keep from creating a dust trail. After guessing, more than once, which fork in the road to take, they found the Qara-Chai River. Following the river to the north, they were able to skirt around Javarseyan and avoid the roadblock.

Back on the pavement, they continued toward the heavy-water nuclear reactor site. Just before reaching the facility's access road, Ari directed, "Sadar, park the vehicle in the shade of this narrow canyon on the right. I hope they won't be able to spot it from the air." As dusk approached, they readied their weapons and surveillance gear for the hike into the nuclear facility. "Okay, we'll need our night vision goggles for this narrow, dark canyon. We must get going. This is going to be a long night."

"Watch for cobras. They are indigenous to this area and it abounds with them. The scorpions will also be out on their nocturnal forage for food and water, and they are just as deadly as the cobras." About that time, a small Persian deer jumped across the trail a few feet in front of them. Startled, and with huge surges of adrenalin running through his veins, Ari raised his UZI and flicked off the safety. Sadar also drew his gleaming Kurdish knife. However, they quickly realized it was a deer and relaxed.

The moon was nearly full during the three-mile hike, and the two operatives reached the top of a hill a half-mile from the nuclear reactor an hour later. They could clearly see the main entrance to the facility in the moonlight glow. "Sadar, you set up the Micro Aerial Vehicles for launching, and I'll ready the notebook computer. I just pray the MAV night vision feature works well. This will be the first time

I've had a chance to try it." He sent two MAVs toward the facility. Watching the split-screen displays on the notebook, Ari exclaimed, "The night vision works great. I can see an owl perched in that tree."

"Yes, and I can hear the crickets chirping over the computer speakers. Look! That sign over the entrance says 'QUATRAN WORKSHOP.' I wonder if they really believe the fake sign will fool anyone."

Ari directed the MAVs to enter the facility as personnel opened the doors. The MAVs were blinded by bright lights inside the facility, so he turned off the night vision feature. "It looks like a change of shifts, with many people coming and going. Look at the size of it! We have the proof that this is a 40-megawatt heavy-water reactor. It takes a lot of people to run this facility."

As Ari took photos and recorded conversations with the MAVs, Sadar declared, "That sign says 'MEDICAL ISOTOPES SECTION.'"

"Of course, that's what the Iranian government claims this reactor is used for. However, the facility is large enough to produce sufficient weapons-grade plutonium to make several nuclear warheads each year. The plutonium is bred from enriched uranium, and only a nuclear reactor can make it in great quantities. They can produce 40 grams of plutonium every single day!" He recalled the MAVs and continued, "We have proof positive now, and we have enough evidence to take out this reactor." Ari immediately uploaded the gathered data and site coordinates to his BlackBerry and transmitted them to Langley. Then he sent a text message to Langley and the team, "*hotel site confirmed soft and good to go. asp.*"

Langley replied, "*asp. get out of there asap. hq.*"

Sadar stored the MAVs when they landed, and then suddenly screamed, "Ieee! A scorpion stung me on the leg!"

Ari rushed over to Sadar, pulled up his pantaloon leg, flicked off the scorpion, and stomped on it. Then he opened his first aid kit and quickly used the snakebite extractor vacuum pump to suck out some of the deadly venom from Sadar's wound. He applied insect bite solution to the area, gave him two antihistamine tablets, and ordered, "Stay calm. We don't want the remaining venom in your system to rush to your heart. I have to get you back to the Land Rover, and then into a hospital for a dose of anti-venom. The nearest medical facility would be at Arak."

"No, No, Ari. We would not make it past the roadblock at Javarseyan, and it would take too much time to detour around the village. You must take me to the Bouali Hospital in Hamadan."

"Okay, my friend. Remember, stay calm." As Ari helped Sadar back to the Land Rover, rain clouds blocked out the moon and tiny rain drops dampened their clothing. Ari stowed the surveillance gear in the vehicle and put Sadar in the front passenger seat. Then, with his UZI cocked and locked on his lap, he sped off toward Hamadan. "I pray we don't attract attention while speeding through the villages in the middle of the night." They did not. The streets were deserted and darkened, and the villagers appeared to be sound asleep.

Approaching Hamadan, Sadar whispered weakly, "Turn left on Bolivar-e-Besat. The hospital is on the southwest side of town. Hurry, my leg hurts and it is swelling up." A moment later, he yelled, "I feel dizzy and nauseous."

"Don't pass out now, my friend. I need more directions."

"Bouali Hospital is on the left, just across from the Bu-Ali Sina University. You cannot miss it."

The Emergency Room doctor immediately gave Sadar an injection of polyvalent scorpion anti-venom and stated, "This will take care of the scorpion venom neurotoxins." Then the doctor gave him an oral antihistamine and a sedative. He put cold packs on his leg, and ordered, "Take the cold packs off when the pain subsides. You must rest in bed for several days. This is critical for your recovery!"

Walking down the hall on the way out of the hospital, Ari noticed Muslim women nursing babies in their rooms, with full breasts exposed in front of male family members and strangers passing by in the hallway. This caused him to ask, "Sadar, why is it that women in Iran must be covered from head to toe when in public, yet they are allowed to expose their bare breasts in front of men while nursing their babies?"

"That, my dear friend, is an anomaly of the Islamic faith. I do not have an answer for you."

Ari drove Sadar to Abraham's villa. Sleepy-eyed, Uncle Abraham greeted the two operatives and served them hot coffee. "I was worried about you. Why are you so late?" Ari related their adventures over the coffee. Ari sent a text message to Langley and the team, "*asp safe at location golf. contact injured.*" Then they retired for a welcome night's sleep in a safe haven.

Day Three continued: Asp

Sadar was still sound asleep when Ari arose at mid-morning. Over a breakfast of bagels, lox, cream cheese, and hot tea, Ari asked Abraham, "May Sadar stay here for awhile? The doctor ordered him to remain in bed for a few days."

"Of course! He may stay until he is strong enough to travel, or as long as he likes. My home is your home, as well as his home."

"Thank you, Uncle Abraham. We are forever in your debt."

When Sadar woke up at mid-day, Ari gave him an envelope containing $5,000 U.S. and said, "Thank you for your brave and untiring dedication to the mission. I must leave, and Abraham will make sure you get home safely when you are well enough to travel. I'll take the Land Rover and drive out of the country before the fireworks start."

"No, no, Ari. You must take me to my family in Sanandaj. They will heal me with herbs in the Kurdish way."

"Okay, my friend. I certainly owe you that much, and even more. You rest today and we'll leave at dawn tomorrow."

Abraham chimed in, "You are welcome to stay here, Sadar. But, I understand your desire to be with your family. Now, you must eat and gain back your strength." The operatives relaxed the rest of the day, and the three men discussed the story of Queen Esther, King Xerxes, Mordecai, and the history of the Jews in Persia. Abraham served a fine meal of hearty beef-barley soup, matzo crackers, Mediterranean-style black olives, fresh carrots, dates, sweet oranges, and coffee that evening. They retired early after saying their prayers in Hebrew.

Day Four continued: Asp

They were up before sunrise the next day. Abraham provided a light breakfast of bagels, goat cheese, oranges, and hot tea. Then he wished the two operatives a safe journey. "Sadar, you may visit me any time you wish. And, my dear nephew, I know you may never return to Persia. *Shalom!* I pray that Yahweh will always be with you."

Ari and Sadar responded, "*Shalom*, Abraham."

Then Ari added, "May Yahweh always protect you, my dear uncle."

Ari made sure Sadar was comfortable in the back seat of the Land Rover. "Let me know anytime you want to stop for a few minutes. Now, you can direct me to the Sanandaj Highway."

"Go west on Bolivar. Then turn right onto the Hamadan-Kermanshah Highway."

"Will do, Sadar."

After Ari drove several miles out of town, Sadar advised, "The Sanandaj Highway is coming up. Turn north here." Ari drove through the village of Bahar and the road veered to the northwest. Entering Qarveh, Sadar suggested, "Take the back streets through the village. Sometimes there is a government roadblock in town on the highway. I do not feel good, Ari." Then he perked up and grinned as he declared, "We are in Kurdistan Province now. This is *my* territory!"

Approaching Sanandaj, Ari asked, "What is that tall peak ahead?"

"Mount Abidar." Pointing to the north, he continued, "Over there is a fortress dating back to the Abbasid period." As Ari drove past the old Sanandaj Bazaar, Sadar commented, "Many of the bazaar merchants here were Jews, at least until the late 1980s. That is when most Jews migrated to Israel because the ruling *mullahs* and the Shias in the populace were not tolerant of them. However, as you know, the Kurds were always tolerant of the Hebrew race."

As Ari approached the Hajar Khatoon Mosque, Sadar instructed, "Turn left at the mosque." Then he directed him to his sister Niyaz's home. Niyaz and her husband, Halmat, welcomed the two travelers. Niyaz immediately tended to Sadar's scorpion wound by placing special herbs over and around the sting area. Meanwhile, Ari sent a text message to

91

Langley and the team, "*asp safe and relocated to undisclosed location. get coordinates from gps signal.*"

Ari then received a text message from Pat, "*asp. meet copperhead at location charlie asap. viper leader.*" Saluting Sadar, he commented, "Well, I'm off to Tabriz."

Niyaz chimed in, "First, as my guest, you must eat." She served a light meal of fresh fruit, nuts, goat cheese, *Nan-e-tafttoon*, and hot tea. Then Ari thanked Niyaz and Halmat for their hospitality.

Halmat warned Ari, "There is an Ansar-e-Hezbollah checkpoint at Saqqez. You have to take the gravel road through the mountains from Iranshah to Takab. Then proceed northwest and drive through Shahindezh to Miandoab. That way you will avoid Saqqez. Your skin is dark, so you will not attract the attention of the villagers along the way."

"Thank you for that warning, my friend. I will heed your advice." The four exchanged *shalom's* and Ari departed for Tabriz. He turned right onto the gravel road at Iranshah and headed east. The road climbed high into the lightly forested Zagros Mountains and Ari thought, *It sure is crisp and cool up here . . . the air is refreshing after being in the stifling desert the past few days.*

At the end of the road, he turned left in the village of Takab. A lone, elderly Kurd villager, armed with an AK-47 assault rifle and a shiny-bladed knife tucked in his cummerbund, eyed Ari warily as he approached. The operative felt a little angst, and adrenalin rushed through his veins as he flipped the safety off on his UZI. He was ready for battle! Then, with a grin that displayed several missing teeth, the Kurd waved him on by. Tremendously relieved, Ari smiled, waved back, and surmised, *Halmat must have got word to him that I was coming this way.*

The gravel road narrowed as he proceeded through a canyon guarded by tall sentinels of snow-capped mountain peaks. Shahindezh appeared deserted as he passed through the tiny mountain village.

Dropping down out of the mountains, Ari viewed the city of Miandoab located in the middle of a large, fertile delta region. He could see the Zarrineh and Simineh rivers feeding the delta, and huge Lake Urmia off in the distance. "What a beautiful sight to behold in parched, God-forsaken Persia!" he exclaimed aloud. As he passed by the burial site of the prophet Zoroaster, humid welcoming warmth, similar to the Israeli coastline, hit him and he mused, *This feels just like the weather back home at Caesarea!*

Ari headed north on the main highway and passed through Bonab and Adjabshir. Then the road went past the eastern shore of Lake Urmia for a few miles. Heading inland again, he drove through Ajarshar. *Good, this is the last leg of the journey to Tabriz. I'm beginning to feel a lot more at ease now,* he contemplated.

The sun was setting over the red-hued mountains as Ari approached Tabriz. He sent a text message to Alev, *"copperhead. arrived and need directions. asp."*

Alev checked the GPS coordinates from Ari's BlackBerry signal and replied, *"asp. meet me at the highway petrol station on south side of town. copperhead."*

While waiting for Alev, Ari gassed up the Land Rover at the petrol station. Then Alev pulled along side his vehicle and nodded. Ari nodded back and followed her to Nader's villa. Inside the home, they greeted each other warmly and Alev introduced him to her cousin and his family. Ari immediately sent Langley and the team a text message, *"asp safe at position charlie."* Then he asked Alev, "What's next?"

She responded, "We wait here for Patrick."

That night, Alev propositioned Ari. He respectfully declined her offer and explained, "I know how interested you are in Patrick. Besides, I'm Orthodox Jew and I shouldn't have sex outside of marriage."

Alev just pouted.

CHAPTER SIX: NATANZ

Farhad is in his mid-forties and dresses neatly in Occidental-style clothing. He displays typical Persian male features: dark skin, medium height, handsome face with a prominent nose, black hair, and black eyes. He was named for a character in Persian poet Ferdowsi's epic piece, *Shahnameh*. Farhad's grandfather was an Iraqi Arab and his grandmother's family roots are with the Bakhtiari tribe in the Zagros Mountains of southwest Iran. She gave up the nomadic life of the Bakhtiaris when she was an adolescent and settled down in Ahvaz with her new husband.

Farhad is a proud man. He is a bachelor, but not by choice; he just cannot find the right woman to marry. He is also a Sunni. However, because only four percent of the nation's population are Sunni Muslim, his faith does not fit in too well with the predominately Shia Muslim families of eligible women. Unless he is prepared to marry a cousin, which he is not, Farhad concludes he will be single the rest of his life.

As a teenager during the 1979 revolution, he harbored strong anti-Shah feelings and even distributed illegal Ayatollah Ruhollah Khomeini audio tapes during the pre-revolution days, as did most teens in the country then. Farhad attended the University of Yazd, majored in architecture and urban planning, and planned to work toward a master's degree after receiving his bachelor's degree. However, he dropped out after his third year because the professors and many of the students expressed strong prejudice toward him and his Sunni faith.

Farhad loves listening to recordings of his favorite Iranian female vocalist, Googoosh, and had listened to her songs all his life. When female singers were banned in Iran after the revolution, he managed to buy her bootlegged CDs at the Bandar-e-Abbas Bazaar. It seems that nearly everything that was illegal in Iran, from liquor to American toys to Levis, could be bought at *that* bazaar. Farhad even crossed the Persian Gulf once, along with thousands of other avid Iranian fans, to attend a live Googoosh performance in Dubai.

He is a member of the Iranian People's Mujahedeen opposition group that seeks to overthrow the current government theocracy and establish a democratic government in Iran. Farhad heard about a proposed CIA-led clandestine mission from his uncle in Ahvaz. Disillusioned with the hard-line incumbent government for many years, and not too happy with his situation in life, he eagerly wanted to volunteer to help. His uncle then put him in touch with a covert CIA agent in Ahvaz and Farhad was instantly recruited for the mission.

Day Three continued: Adder

A *muezzin's* daybreak call to prayer from the Friday Mosque woke Logan and Farhad. Logan commented, "If I remember correctly, this is the first of five calls to prayer each day."

"You are correct. Good Muslims kneel on small prayer rugs and face Mecca when they pray to Allah five times a day. We call it the *panz namez.*"

Farhad's cousin, Amir, served them a light breakfast of hot Caspian *chahee* and biscuits with honey. The two operatives were soon out the door and heading to the uranium enrichment site north of Natanz. Farhad drove the Mercedes past the old Jogand Caravansary on the Ardestan-Naan Road and went through the Zavareh Village district. "Did you know that Ardestan is an ancient city that was founded during the Sassanid era?"

"No I didn't, Farhad. However, I assumed it was a centuries old settlement because it *looks* very old. Wasn't the Sassanian Dynasty the last of the pre-Islamic Persian Empires? I believe they controlled the region during the third through seventh centuries A.D."

"Yes, it was. Those four hundred years were one of Persia's most important and most influential periods."

After passing by several mosques, they headed northwest out of town. The road paralleled the barren Karkas Mountain Range to the west, which was dotted with occasional clumps of low brush and rock formations. The arid *Dasht-e-Kavir*, with its scorching sands and hot winds, was to the east of the highway. Mirages in the wilderness looked like welcome, cooling lakes through the shimmering heat waves. As they proceeded, the road made a sharp turn to the southwest at the cross-country railroad tracks. Farhad then turned north on the Natanz-Kashan Road and drove toward the town of Natanz. The temperature was a searing 118 degrees and they ran the air conditioner to keep from roasting. Farhad drove by pear and pomegranate orchards just outside of the city. He offered, "With the abundant water from the nearby mountains running through the *qanats*, this is a prime fruit-growing area." It was about a thirty-five mile drive from Ardestan to Natanz.

"Farhad, what's that domed, sand-colored octagon structure on top of the mountain above us?"

"That is the Baz Dome. It is a monument built during the reign of Shah Abbas, and it is considered to be a masterpiece of Persian architecture." Bare-topped men, hitting their own chests and backs with steel chains and drawing blood, filled the town's main boulevard. The sounds of the participants' lamentations nearly drowned out the musical cadence of wind instruments and drums that they were marching to the beat of. "This is a Shia ritual of self-flagellation. It is really an act of religious mortification

97

and commemorates the Battle of Karbala, which is in present-day Iraq. That is where Hussein, grandson of the Prophet Mohammed, was martyred in 680 AD. Of course, we Sunnis do not believe in the ritual."

"Yes. I remember when Shah Pahlavi outlawed the inhumane practice. The Islamic Republic must approve and encourage it now."

"That is right, Logan, and the ruling *mullahs* took the country right back to the seventh century, or at least to the Dark Ages."

"If I remember my Islamic history correctly, it was the Sunnis that killed the Shiite leader, Hussein."

"Logan, you remember your history lesson very well. We were the ones the Shias were fighting in Karbala, and we are still fighting each other today."

"Look! There's a large group of young women in colorful *chadors* marching behind the men."

"That is a more recent development. Sometimes the female participants even turn the event into a street party! Of course, the *mullahs* in Tehran do not like that."

"You know the town. Let's detour around this mess."

"Will do, Logan. Any roadblock guards will be more interested in the ritual parade than in us." Farhad took a side street and drove past Kouhab Castle. "Shah Abbas built that castle as a caravansary. And look, those stone and mortar ruins are the remains of the Koushk Fire Temple." While passing through the Arisman Village district, he continued, "This ancient village within Natanz is 6,000-years-old."

"Egad! In England, we think anything 1,000-years-old is bloody ancient."

Leaving the city, Farhad headed north. "It is not far now, just ahead on the left. In this bare countryside with just low foothills for cover, how will we get close to the target?"

Logan replied, "Continue on past the main paved road that goes to the uranium enrichment center. We'll look for a place to hide the vehicle while I figure out a plan."

A mile or so north of the nuclear facility access road, Farhad spotted a dry creek crossing the highway. "I think I can drive the Mercedes to the west up this *wadi*."

"Okay, let's try it. Drive very slow so we don't create a dust trail . . . or break an axle." When they were around a bend in the dry creek and out of sight of the highway, Logan advised, "Stop here and I'll get my bearings."

"This topographical map of the area should help."

"The topo map is a great help. Good thinking, Farhad." Logan used the GPS feature on his BlackBerry to determine their exact location. Then he quickly developed a route, via natural depressions and dry creek beds, to a low knoll about a mile from the nuclear site. "Let's grab the surveillance gear and our weapons. We can hike in from here."

"In this heat? I believe we should wait until dusk when it is not so hot."

"Farhad, you're well acclimated to the extreme heat, and I've been on prolonged desert treks in this region before. We can do it. Just take extra water and we'll wear our Arab *djellabas* and *keffiyahs* for protection from the brutal sun. Besides, it's too hot for the indigenous Persian Horned Desert Viper to be foraging for food and water now, so this is the safest time for our hike."

"Okay, you are the boss. Besides, one bite from that snake and you are a dead man!"

Loaded down with Logan's UZI, Farhad's AK-47, spare loaded magazines for their weapons, the notebook computer, the Micro Aerial Vehicles, and plenty of water, they began the arduous ordeal in the blistering sun. Heat waves rose from the desert floor, and every breath of air seemed hot and stifling. The overheated and exhausted operatives finally reached their objective two hours later. Farhad broke off some low growing clumps of brush and suggested, "We should put some of this in our headgear to break up our silhouettes."

"Good idea. Then we'll be less likely to be spotted." They crawled to the top of the knoll for a peek at the Natanz Uranium Enrichment Center located at the foot of the Karkas Mountains. "Farhad, keep your head down and help me scan the complex with your binoculars. Let's locate the entrances to the underground fuel enrichment centrifuge chambers."

"Okay. I see security forces all over the area. I hope they do not see us."

"Those three unnatural-looking low sand mounds seem suspicious. There are too many workers going in and out of the buildings in front of them, so that must be how they access the underground centrifuge chambers. I'll take telephotos of the area, and then we'll check out the building interiors with the MAVs."

"This is a huge complex, Logan. There must be more than twenty buildings here."

"This is Iran's main uranium centrifuge enrichment site. It contains a Pilot Fuel Enrichment Plant, and a complete Fuel Enrichment Plant with three large underground sections. Set up the MAVs while I ready the computer." Logan sent three MAVs in the direction of the cluster of buildings. "We'll check out the building in front of the largest mound first." He perched two MAVs on the roof to save their batteries and directed one to follow personnel into the structure. "The subterranean chambers reportedly hold cascades with 50,000 centrifuges."

"Yes. The Iranian People's Mujahedeen opposition group, which is controlled by The National Council for the Resistance of Iran, discovered this facility as well as the heavy-water plant at Arak. They brought the two locations to the attention of international weapons inspectors. I know, because I was involved in both discoveries. We are an anti-government group because we believe that the Iranian people are hostages of the ruling *mullahs* in Tehran"

"Farhad, that information was in your dossier. I also know you're a member of the Mujahedeen, and that's why you were accepted for this mission." Logan sent the MAV down a flight of stairs, along a well-lit tunnel, and into a huge hall-like room. He scanned the area and exclaimed, "Those heaters are the beginning of the gas centrifuge process."

"Look. The containers next to the heaters are labeled U-235 in Persian!"

"They contain natural, solid U-235 yellowcake uranium. When it melts, hexafluoride gas fills and pressurizes the containers. The gas is then fed into cascades of rotating cylinders, and a stream of slightly enriched U-235 is withdrawn and fed into the next higher stage, and so forth. At the end of the process, UF6 gas is cooled and solidified to obtain enriched uranium." *I certainly hope that overview wasn't too technical for him.*

"I see. What happens next?"

"The enriched uranium is sent to a fuel fabrication plant to be converted into fuel assemblies for nuclear reactors. Low enriched uranium is used for nuclear fuel. However, highly enriched uranium is used for nuclear weapons."

"I understand, Logan."

"I've seen enough of this one. Let's determine if the other suspect mounds contain more centrifuge cascades." Logan then directed the MAV outside, and sent all three to

101

the next building where he parked two of them. He sent a fresh one into the structure, and then into another large hall-like underground room.

Looking at the computer screen, Farhad commented, "This room looks identical to the first one."

"That's right, except on a slightly smaller scale. There's not as many bloody cascades here. Let's check out the third mound." He sent the MAVs to the next building and directed a fresh one inside. "This underground cascade hall is set up the same as the other two. I'll retrieve the MAVs and you can pack them up while I send the data to the CIA."

"Will do. What is that other large building near the mounds?"

"Our Intel indicates it contained the original centrifuge cascades used before they decided to go underground." He contemplated, *The bloke is certainly bright!*

Logan uploaded the photos, data, and site coordinates to his BlackBerry and transmitted them to Langley. Then he sent Langley and the team a text message, "*kilo site confirmed soft and good to go. adder.*"

Langley replied, "*adder. get out of there asap. hq.*"

Logan folded up the notebook and said, "Let's get going before we're seen."

"Right behind you. Whew, it must be 125 degrees now! I am baking in the sun."

"Slow down, take it easy, and just sip your water. You'll be okay. Look at the dark clouds over the mountains . . . that should cool you down. I can even see occasional lightning strikes up there."

"Rain in the mountains can also cause flash flooding down here, Logan."

The intense heat slowed them down and it took a little longer to hike back to the Mercedes. Farhad started the engine and stated, "I am turning on the air conditioner to cool us down because I feel sick from the heat."

"I do too. However, the symptoms will pass when our body temperatures drop back down close to normal."

Farhad slowly eased the vehicle along the *wadi* toward the highway. Then he yelled, "Flashflood!"

Logan looked out the rear window and saw a four-foot wall of water rushing down the dry creek bed toward them. He hollered, "Get out of this *wadi* now, now, now!"

Farhad gunned the motor, spinning the tires on smooth river rock. Then he pulled up a slight embankment as the fast moving water below them took everything in its path downstream. He exclaimed, "*Merci*, Allah! That was certainly a close call."

"Very close, my friend. Extremely close. The bloody torrent would have washed us away."

Farhad continued slowly across the soft sand on the desert floor until they reached the highway. As they headed south toward Natanz, Farhad asked, "What if we get stopped at the checkpoint in town?"

"Let's pray that the flagellation ritual parade is still in progress and the guards won't notice us. I'll tell you one thing though; we'll shoot our way through a checkpoint if necessary. Those bloody heathens aren't going to behead me like they did me father!"

"What! What do you mean, Logan?"

"Me pop was working as a contractor on the installation of British telephone switching equipment in the Holy city of Qom when I was a young lad. Me mum told me he got into a minor traffic accident in the city and two bloody Iranians in the other vehicle barbarically beheaded Pop, and then put his head on the hood of his company car!"

"That is horrific ... they must have been Shiites. I know that Sunnis would not commit such an inhuman act today."

"The blokes were of the Shia faith. One was a *mullah*, the other was a xenophobic layman, and they both believed they would be assured a place in Paradise if they killed an infidel in the name of Allah."

"Do you know what happened to them?"

"I certainly do! While on a covert MI6 assignment in Qom many years ago, I tracked down the two culprits and settled the score. I believe the bloody suckers are in Hades now, instead of their version of Paradise. I've never told this story to anyone before, except me mum. Bless her departed soul."

"Logan, that happened when I was very young. However, the tale is still told about their misdeed, and their mysterious disappearance. Now I know the whole story. They deserved what ever you did to them."

As they entered the north side of Natanz, Farhad exclaimed, "We are in trouble now! The ritual parade is over and the main boulevard is nearly deserted."

"Let's try a side street. Maybe we'll get lucky and not be spotted as we pass through town." Farhad headed south on a parallel street. About halfway across the town, Logan looked down a cross street and spotted an Ansar-e-Hezbollah roadblock on the main boulevard. One of the *Hezbollahi* guards pointed at them. Logan yelled, "Step on it! They've seen us."

Farhad floor-boarded the Mercedes and weaved around donkey carts and pedestrians in front of the Natanz Bazaar. "I am turning left onto this side street. We have to get back on the highway and try to outrun them." He clipped a cooked beet stand on the corner, sending the vendor, his charcoal grill, several huge hot beets, and the community knife and fork flying into the *jube*. As he turned right onto the main boulevard, a Hezbollah vehicle rear-ended the Mercedes. Farhad lost control of his vehicle and plowed into a lorry parked directly across the street from the train station.

With steam pouring out of the radiator and their vehicle disabled, Logan yelled, "Lock and load! Get out and take cover." The two operatives crouched behind the Mercedes as they took fire from three *Hezbollahi* guards shooting at them with AK-47 full-auto assault rifles. They returned fire, Logan with his 9-millimeter UZI submachine gun set on full-auto, and Farhad with his 7.62-millimeter AK-47 assault carbine. The *Hezbollahis* peppered the Mercedes with dozens of 7.62-millimeter rounds, some of them penetrating completely through both sides of the vehicle. Logan took out two of them with his UZI.

Another Hezbollah vehicle with three heavily armed men screeched to a halt near the other adversary. Farhad shouted, "Logan, we do not have a prayer of getting out of this alive!"

"I'll trigger the self-destruct features built into the notebook computer and MAV cases to destroy our findings." He pushed a speed-dial button on his BlackBerry and the resulting explosions popped open the boot of the Mercedes. Smoke poured out and the vehicle caught on fire. As Logan made a tactical reload on his UZI, he shouted, "This is my last magazine!"

"I am almost out of ammo also!" screamed Farhad. Suddenly, ten Mujahedeen commandos joined in the firefight to help the desperate operatives. "Those are my colleagues. They knew about our mission and they have come to help us. Praises to Allah!"

"Amen!" Logan hollered. The Mujahedeen easily wiped out all of the Hezbollah guards after an exchange of gunfire. Then a group of commandos drove up the street to make sure there were not any guards left at the checkpoint.

Glancing toward Farhad, Logan saw him slumped over a twenty-kilo burlap sack full of potatoes. Logan hollered, "What the bloody hell! Farhad, are you okay?" Getting no answer, he ran over to him and saw that his face was ashen, he was gasping for air, and blood was squirting out of multiple chest and neck wounds. "Oh, no, my dear friend." Logan tried to stop the bleeding, but it was too late.

With what appeared to be a peaceful twinkle in his eyes, Farhad barely whispered, "Now . . . I am going to Paradise," as he expired. The Mujahedeen leader said, in broken English, "Me Abbas. We take care of our brother." Gesturing toward a vehicle, he continued, "Now, come with us. You drive Hezbollah machine."

Logan drove south through Ardestan and toward Yazd in one of the Hezbollah vehicles. He had two carloads of Mujahedeen commandos escorting him, one in the lead and one in the rear. They put him up in a safe house at Yazd, and Abbas remarked, "Thank you for what you do for us. You eat and sleep now."

Logan handed Abbas an envelope containing $5,000 U.S. and said, "Please see that Farhad's family receives this. He was a valiant and loyal operative."

Abbas nodded as they shook hands and he replied, "No problem, I do it. *Merci, Aga.*"

Logan then sent a text message to Langley and the team, "*adder safe and relocated to undisclosed location. get coordinates from gps signal. contact deceased.*"

Langley replied, *adder. it's done. hq.*"

CHAPTER SEVEN: ISFAHAN

Farah is a lovely, demure woman in her early forties. Her smooth brown complexion, brunette hair with a hint of curls, shamrock-green eyes, and pleasant demeanor attracts many men. Moreover, she lacks the prominent Persian nose that is typical of most Iranians, and this facial feature enhances her beauty. Her mother named her after Shah Pahlavi's attractive wife, Queen Farah. As a mature woman, she is every bit as beautiful as the deposed queen was. Her father passed away a few years ago, and she lives with her mother.

Farah had several suitors in the past, but every one of them was overbearing and displayed the usual Persian trait of male dominance. With a very few exceptions, the men seemed to agree with the *mullahs* in charge of the current Islamic regime that females should always be covered head to toe while in public. Her suitors also could not accept the concept of the same freedoms for women that men enjoyed. She vehemently disagreed with their views on anti-feminine rights.

A descendant of the Qashqai tribe and a Shia Muslim, Farah is proud of her heritage. Although always covered while out in public, she usually wears colorful, airy Qashqai veils. However, she does wear black *chadors* while in the capital city of Tehran and the Holy cities of Qom and Mashad.

Farah attended the vast University of Isfahan, where she majored in literature and earned a Bachelor of Arts degree in Humanities and Literature. While in college, she became active in an illegal women's rights society. Her domineering boyfriend disapproved of the movement, so their relationship did not last very long. She still attends

107

monthly clandestine meetings with the group to discuss the government's latest attempts to suppress all female rights in Iran. Farah is also an accomplished pianist. However, she is forbidden to perform before men in public, as are all women in Iran. Therefore, she plays only for family gatherings and at her women's rights society meetings.

Farah loves Persia, but she is not too happy with her place in life and prays for a change in the government. The recent presidential election offered a ray of hope for such a change, but she believed that the results were manipulated when the popular candidate was defeated. Of course, she was one of the demonstrators rioting over the election results in the streets of Isfahan. Government prosecutors of detained demonstrators called the unrest "… an attempt by Western nations, particularly the United States and Britain, to inspire a 'velvet revolution.'" She also admires the female leader of the Iranian People's Mujahedeen, Maryam Rajavi, who lives in Paris with her husband.

Farah gladly accepted the opportunity to be part of the covert mission when she heard about it from her women's rights society members. Moreover, she was elated upon discovering she would be her dear friend, Zivah's, local contact.

Day Two continued: Cobra

Zivah awoke after a peaceful night dreaming about being with Patrick. Farah's mother prepared a typical Persian breakfast consisting of fried eggs, *nan e lavash*, goat cheese, butter, rosehip flavored pomegranate jam, walnuts, and hot *chahee*. "That was delicious! Your mother is a great hostess, Farah. Now it's time to drive to the university campus and check-out the Isfahan Administration Offices."

"Okay, I am ready to do some spying. Here is an attractive Qashqai veil for you to wear. With your dark complexion, you will blend right in with the rest of the women on the campus."

Farah drove her Paykan west to the Isfahan Bazaar in the city center, and then skirted around Royal Square and headed south on Chahar Baq Abbasi Avenue. "Hey, that's the caravansary-style Ali Qapu Hotel. Do you remember when I stayed there during my last trip to Isfahan?"

"Yes. I recall that you were in the shower one evening and you had shampoo in your hair when the hotel water was turned off." Farah laughed and continued, "I knocked on all the doors of the rooms on your floor until I collected enough bottled water to rinse the suds out of your hair, and the soap off your beautiful naked body!"

"That was really something! I finally learned to expect the unexpected in Iran and not to linger in the shower."

Farah drove down Charhar Baq Bala Avenue and onto the University of Isfahan property. "Oh, Oh! Look at the campus security patrols. What do we do now, Zivah?"

"Just drive as if we belong here. They won't stop two properly attired women."

Farah parked behind a large, gray stone building. "Ara, the daughter of one of my women's rights society members, lives in this dormitory. It is just across from the main building of the Isfahan Administration Offices, and her third floor window faces the structure. She offered to let us use her room as long as we need it. Of course, she is not aware of what we will be doing there, nor is she aware of the potential outcome of the mission."

"That's good. The fewer outsiders who know about our mission, the safer our task will be. Let's take our gear upstairs."

Packed in cardboard boxes as if they were moving into the dorm, the two operatives carried the Micro Aerial Vehicles, notebook computer, and binoculars up the three

109

flights of stairs. Zivah's 9-millimeter UZI submachine gun and her holstered 9-millimeter SIG pistol, and Farah's 9-millimeter Sten submachine gun, were hidden under their full-length veils. Farah had inherited the World War II vintage Sten from her grandfather, and its weight and muzzle velocity were comparable to the UZI. However, the UZI's 600-rounds-per-minute rate of fire slightly exceeded the Sten's 500 rounds-per-minute. "This is Ara's room. She is ill and is staying at her mother's home in Shah-Reza to the south, but I have the key."

Staying in the shadows of the dorm room so they would not be seen by inquisitive eyes, the operatives unpacked their gear. Zivah took photos of the building exterior, and then she booted the notebook as Farah carefully set two MAVs on the windowsill. "Okay, Farah, I'm launching them and I'll direct them to follow that group of people heading toward the main entrance of the building. We believe this is where the leading scientific brains of the Iranian nuclear weapons program are located."

Watching the group with binoculars, Farah announced excitedly, "You may not recognize him, but that heavy-set man with the bald head is Doctor Ali Kermani. He is an agent for VEVAK, the Iranian Secret Police, and he has a terrifying reputation of enjoying the torturing of prisoners. You probably know, VEVAK, the Ministry of Intelligence and Security, is the successor of the Shah's SAVAK agency, and it is the most powerful ministry in Iran."

"Yes I do, and I've heard about Doctor Kermani. Although I'm not afraid of him and wouldn't hesitate to take him out, we certainly want to stay out of his way and try to avoid a confrontation."

The two MAVs followed Kermani and his group into the Administration Offices. Once inside the secured building and out of range of normal remote listening devices, the group began chatting with each other. Kermani spoke as if he was giving them an overview of the nuclear research offices and facilities, "We are proud of our light-water and heavy-water reactors, which were supplied by Red China. Those facilities are off-campus, and we will visit them later. This building we are in houses the core of our nuclear weapons research and development program, and the security is so tight, no one could *ever* penetrate it."

"That's what you think, Doctor Kermani!" Zivah and Farah both whispered.

A member of the visitor group asked about other weapons-related development and Kermani replied, "Isfahan is the location of our nation's largest ballistic missile production plant. It is a huge facility that the North Koreans helped us build. The city also has one of Iran's major chemical weapons development plants, where we proudly manufacture nerve, blister, blood, and choking agents. So, you see why we are not afraid of the West."

"Farah, let's check out that area to the left. If my Persian comprehension is correct, the sign says, 'ZIRCONIUM PRODUCTION RESEARCH GROUP.'"

"You are correct, Zivah."

"Zirconium is used to produce cladding for nuclear fuel. Look, there's several Chinese in the group, and I'll bet they are nuclear scientists. I'll record their conversations and let Langley do the translations."

"The scientists in this other group are talking about a 100-Watt Heavy-Water Zero Power Reactor. And, it sounds like those other scientists are working on final plans for underground nuclear research facilities just outside the city."

"Farah, this building is the heart of Iran's nuclear development program. Therefore, it must go. Of course, we won't use bunker-busters here, but I hope an air strike with smart bombs doesn't take out any innocent students."

111

"I can help there. My women's rights society will secretly pass the word to the students and they will *not* be on campus the day of the air strike."

"Good. I understand we also have an *Irani* mole inside. Langley will have to warn him as well."

"So, we have a spy inside!"

"I'm recalling the MAVs. Pack them up as soon as they land on the window sill." Zivah immediately uploaded the photos, data, and site coordinates to her BlackBerry and transmitted them to Langley. Then she sent Langley and the team a text message, *"lima one site confirmed soft and good to go. cobra."*

Langley replied, *"cobra. check out lima two tomorrow. hq."*

As Zivah folded up the notebook she said, "Okay, let's get out of here."

The two operatives took their time driving off the campus and back to Farah's villa so they would not raise suspicions. Then they dined on *nan-e-tafttoon* and *beryani-biryani*, a traditional Isfahan ground lamb dish cooked on one side in a small pan over an open fire. For dessert, they enjoyed servings of sweet *khoresht-e-mast*, another traditional Isfahan dish made with lamb stew, yogurt, saffron, sugar, and orange rinds. "What a feast, Farah. I complement your mother for her hospitality and for her exceptional culinary skills."

Farah's mother tipped her head to one side in the Persian fashion and replied, "Thank you, My Precious Guest. May Allah bless you."

"Farah, we'll check-out the Isfahan Nuclear Technology and Research Center in the morning. Let's get a good night's sleep now." Zivah again dreamt about Patrick throughout the night.

Day Three continued: Cobra

Over a light breakfast of thick, fresh *nan-e-bahr-bahr-ee*, tangy goat cheese, and hot Caspian *chahee*, Farah discussed the plans for the day with Zivah. "There is no way we can get close enough to the huge INTRC complex to utilize the MAVs. It is at the base of barren Soteh Mountain and the Iranian Revolutionary Guard security is incredible in that area. Therefore, I arranged for fake janitorial identification cards so we can freely access the buildings. Two of the cleaning women are calling in sick today, and we will be their replacements. Security patrols will not pay much attention to menial cleaning women covered head to toe with black *chadors*."

"Good plan," Zivah responded. "What about accessing the underground facilities?"

"That's a different story. Cleaning crews are not allowed into the top secret underground locations."

"It will be a challenge then. We'll leave our submachine guns here because security forces may spot them. However, I'll conceal my 9-millimeter SIG and a few spare magazines underneath my *chador*."

Farah drove her Pakan past Vank Church in the Jolfa district. "Look, Zivah, do you remember seeing this beautiful Christian church in the Armenian neighborhood?"

"Of course, and I especially recall the fine religious oil paintings with their gilded frames. I'm surprised Iran's hard-core Islamic rulers haven't destroyed all the Christian churches in the country."

"Yes, and I am surprised all of the Armenians did not leave Iran after the revolution, like most of the Jews did. Christians and Jews are not treated very well here. Maybe the *mullahs* believe they must preserve religious works of art, so they leave the churches alone."

"I want to tell you about the gorgeous hunk of a man in charge of our mission. His name is Patrick and, although he's an Irish Catholic, I can't stop thinking about him day and night."

"Tell me more. What does he look like, and what kind of personality does he have? Can you really get serious about someone outside of your faith?"

"Patrick is in his late-forties, but young looking. He looks like Adonis, the handsome young man in Greek mythology. He's a trim six feet tall, with curly black hair, seductive hazel eyes, and a slightly dark complexion. I think I'm in love, or at least I'm infatuated with him, and I'll face the religion dilemma when and if it's necessary."

"Dear, dear Zivah, I certainly pray it works out for you."

Farah continued driving southeast toward the mountains until they left the metropolitan area. She explained, "The INTRC is part of the University of Isfahan. It employs over 3,000 scientists, plus a large support staff. Moreover, it is a multi-purpose research center, with numerous large buildings located on Iran's largest nuclear research complex."

Zivah added, "The site contains a 30-Kilowatt Miniaturized Neutron Source Reactor, a Light-water Sub-critical Reactor, and a laboratory scale 100-Watt Heavy-water Zero Power Reactor. They were installed with the help of Red Chinese nuclear experts. A hexafluoride conversion plant facility and a zirconium cladding plant, plus other laboratories and facilities, are co-located on the site."

Farah added, "And, it is well fortified with anti-aircraft missile systems."

As the operatives approached the site, Zivah continued, "The INTRC is listed as an entity of concern for proliferation of nuclear weapons by the Japanese government. It's also listed as an entity of potential concern for weapons of mass destruction-related procurement by the British government. And, just recently, the American government said it has serious concerns that Iran is deliberately attempting to preserve their nuclear weapons option."

"I understand. The 150-acre Isfahan Uranium Conversion Facility is also on this site, and our hard-core leaders in Tehran are certainly up to quite a few nefarious activities."

"Yes, Farah. That's a large-scale conversion facility for processing yellowcake into uranium oxide, uranium hexafluoride, and uranium metal. It supplies U02 uranium dioxide fuel for the 40-MW Heavy-water Reactor at Arak, and UF6 uranium hexafluoride for the Natanz Enrichment Facility. As of 2006, 118 tons of UF6, plus intermediate products, were produced and declared to the International Atomic Energy Agency by Iran. Our Intel indicates that Iran has produced many, many more nuclear products since then."

Iranian Revolutionary Guards on the main gate thoroughly inspected the operatives' papers and identification cards. Then they ordered the women to uncover their faces so they could compare them to the ID photographs. Satisfied with the documents, they gave Farah a car pass and waved the operatives on through the gate.

"Wow, that was really unnerving. I am perspiring from head to toe."

"So am I, Farah, so am I. Look at that tunnel entrance just north of the Uranium Conversion Facility. The IAEA discovered and inspected the long tunnel during 2004, but it was empty then. I'll bet it's not empty now!"

"I believe you are correct. I can see three entrances to the tunnel, each about a half-kilometer apart."

115

"I see them. I'll take some telephoto shots of the area. You know Iran declared that the tunnel is for storage, production, and other activities related to the Uranium Conversion Facility. However, that's baffling because the adjacent Zirconium Production Plant is between the tunnel entrances and the Uranium Conversion Facility. What do they really do in there? I wish we could get in the tunnel, either in person or with our MAVs. We'll try to work out a plan."

"Zivah, we need to check-in at the janitorial office and pick up our cleaning assignments for the day. I believe it is in that small structure between the two large buildings on the right."

Farah and Zivah picked up a list of their assigned duties for the day, as well as a golf cart-like truck, and headed for their first stop. Zivah exclaimed, "Would you believe it? Our first chore is cleaning up the men's room in the Heavy-water Reactor laboratory!"

Farah shook her head in disgust and replied, "*Kharahb!*"

"Yes, it does sound like an awful chore, but we need to check out that lab."

They parked the vehicle behind the laboratory and checked-in with the guard on the rear door. He read their work orders and, grinning from ear-to-ear, offered, "I am going to the men's room and will be happy to show you the way."

There were several workers using the urinals inside the men's room, and Farah whispered in Zivah's ear, "What ever you do, do not look at the men in here, or they may try to take advantage of you."

The security guard eyed the two women wearing head-to-toe black *chadors*, hoping they would glance his way while he stood at the urinals. Of course, they did not. He left

116

the men's room, without washing his hands. Zivah let out a sigh of relief and thought, *Iranian men are something else!*

After completing their distasteful cleaning chore, the operatives headed for their second assigned task, mopping the floor around the small Heavy-water Reactor. There were about two dozen white-smocked nuclear scientists working near the reactor. Farah asked quietly, "Why do they want the floors mopped during the day, instead of at night when there are fewer workers around?"

"Probably because, for security, they don't want cleaning crews alone in the facility at night," Zivah answered in a hushed tone. "Look, there's a group of Chinese scientists over there. Let's start cleaning the floor where they're standing. Maybe we'll pick up some tidbits of information." The operatives diligently mopped around the Chinese group, occasionally slopping a wet mop over their shoes.

Out of normal hearing range, Farah said under her breath, "They are speaking the Mandarin dialect and no one is interpreting the discussion into Persian. It is too bad they are not speaking Cantonese, Zivah, because I know a few words and phrases of that dialect."

"Well, our Intel sources believe this is the miniaturized version of a neutron source reactor that the People's Republic of China supplied to Iran, so that group must be the technical experts. This type of reactor is used to breed plutonium on a laboratory scale and we've proven that it exists. It must be taken out. Let's finish up here and get on to the next work assignment."

"That would be the Uranium Conversion Facility. It is just a few blocks away." They checked in with the guard at the service entrance. He reviewed their IDs and work orders, and then directed them to the yellowcake storage area. The department supervisor gave them protective masks and white smocks to wear over their *chadors*. While

117

mopping the floors and dusting the equipment, Farah quietly commented, "I am *gharm!*"

"With three layers of clothing, I'm also hot. It's a good thing that the air conditioning is on in here," Zivah responded. "Farah! Don't touch or get too close to those drums of yellowcake . . . it's radioactive. The drums contain milled uranium oxide powder that will be converted into uranium hexafluoride. Then it will be shipped to Natanz to be enriched into nuclear fuel."

Farah jumped back from the drum she was about to brush off with her duster. "Thanks for the warning. I will stay away from them."

"We have proof that this building contains the starting process of the nuclear fuel cycle. After the uranium yellowcake is converted into UF6 hexafluoride gas it will be enriched for use in nuclear bomb making."

"So, the UF6 might be stored in the tunnels that go deep into the mountain . . . to protect it from air strikes?"

"That's right, Farah, and those nearby storage tanks probably contain recently produced UF6. This is enough proof for me, and I believe the entire complex must be destroyed, including the zirconium plant and the heavy-water reactor. I'll take photos and get accurate GPS coordinates during our janitorial rounds, and then transmit them to Langley."

"What about the tunnels?"

"Of course, the tunnels and any underground facilities have to be destroyed with bunker-buster bombs, followed by commando raids to ensure total destruction. We must try to get close enough to one of the entrances to launch our MAVs and see what's inside the tunnels, and that is the problem. We'll hike up the east side of the mountain to the peak early tomorrow morning and check out the terrain."

"Soteh Mountain looks very stark from here on the west side . . . I do not see any cover at all. It is an impossible task."

"We'll see." As the operatives completed their janitorial duties, Zivah secretly took photos of the main buildings and registered their GPS coordinates.

After they left the INTRC complex at the end of the day, Zivah stated, "I'll send the data we collected when we're far away from peering eyes and prying ears." They stopped at a quiet area on the banks of the Zayandeh River before reaching the Isfahan metropolitan area. She transmitted the photos and site coordinates they obtained to Langley with her BlackBerry. Then she sent Langley and the team a text message, *"lima two site confirmed soft, plus a hardened tunnel, and good to go. follow-up tomorrow. cobra."*

Langley replied, *"cobra. only if necessary. be careful. hq."*

Nearing the downtown district, Farah exclaimed, "Look! People are demonstrating in Royal Square and it looks like the huge crowd goes all the way up to the Isfahan Bazaar. We will have to detour around the city center."

"What in the world is going on? I can see tear gas dispersing the mass of humanity."

"This was supposed to be an Islamic hard-liner rally. However, it looks like reformist opposition supporters are protesting the government-sponsored event. Some of my friends may be protesting, but we want to stay out of the fracas." The operatives bypassed the demonstrators and safely arrived at Farah's villa.

Walking into the dining room, Farah shouted in a delightful tone, *"Mamaa,* you decorated the table for *Now-Ruz.* It is very beautiful!" The New Year table was elaborate and full of colored eggs, candies, fancy sweets, candles, and fresh flowers. There was a mirror set on the exquisite, colorful linen tablecloth. Farah explained, "This is the first day of our two-week Persian New Year celebration."

"I remember. The festive secular tradition is much different than the usual Iranian holidays, which commemorate the deaths of Islamic saints."

"Sadly enough, you are correct about our holy days. However, this is a non-religious Persian tradition that dates back as far as our recorded history. Let us eat now, and we will open *Now-Ruz* gifts after our meal."

The two operatives sat upon a colorful Persian carpet on the floor, and Farah's mother served goat head soup for the festive occasion. As she ladled the spicy broth, she placed one of the eyeballs in Zivah's bowl and exclaimed, "This is for our honored guest."

While on an assignment in Tunisia, Zivah had received a sheep eyeball from an Arab Sheik during a meal, and she was expected to eat the delicacy while everyone watched her. Taking a deep breath, she deftly spooned the eyeball out of the broth, faked chewing the morsel, and swallowed it whole. The family squealed in delight as Zivah smiled and said, "That was delicious!" Then she quickly washed it down with large sips of *chahee*.

After dinner, Farah gave Zivah a gold coin, and a gold necklace with her name written from right to left in Persian. She then said, "These are my family's *Now Ruz* gifts to you. May you have a long life."

Zivah responded with a heartfelt, "*Enshallah! Merci,* my dear friends." Her God Willing and Thank You responses were well received by Farah and her mother.

That night, Zivah tossed and turned as she worried about the undertaking in the morning. *How are we going to get close enough to the tunnel to use the MAVs? This is going to be the most dangerous part of my mission. The Iranian Revolutionary Guards may capture us. I may never see Patrick again!* Eventually, she fell asleep and had restless dreams of being with Patrick during a firefight.

Day Four continued: Cobra

Zivah and Farah were up before dawn. They took a large piece of *bahr-bahr-ee* bread, some goat cheese, several oranges, a handful of white mulberries, a bag of mixed nuts, and four tiny cucumbers from the kitchen. Then they donned black headscarves before leaving the villa.

The pre-dawn streets were deserted as they drove east out of the city on the Isfahan-Nain Highway while munching on their breakfast. A few miles past Soteh Mountain, Farah turned south on a secondary road. A rooster crowed and startled them as they went past a farmhouse. "I am sure nervous," Farah commented.

"Me too. We'd better control our emotions for this important task." Zivah used her BlackBerry GPS to determine their coordinates and to estimate when they were directly opposite the INTRC tunnel on the other side of the mountain. "Pull into this small ravine on the right. We'll hide the car with brush and hike up the mountain from here."

Toting their surveillance gear and submachine guns, the two operatives hiked up the backside of Soteh Mountain in the early morning twilight. The sun started to rise across the Central Plateau, and sparse brush on the barren mountain made it relatively easy to find good footing as they followed zig zagging game trails up the extremely steep slope.

Skirting around a large clump of chaparral, Zivah held up a clenched fist. Farah stopped in her tracks, and then peeked around the bush. They stared in awe at a leopard feasting on a downed Persian Ibex. The leopard eyed the two women, gave out a low warning growl, and continued eating its prey. Zivah whispered, "Let's back away very slowly and, what ever you do, don't turn your back on the beast." They gave the leopard a wide berth and continued their hike up the precipitous mountain.

Approaching the summit, Farah warned, "We had better stay low on this barren ridge."

"Yes. Let's crawl the last few feet to the top and we'll peer over the ridgeline." Looking down the west side of the mountain with binoculars, the operatives observed employees entering the various buildings. A half-dozen security vehicles drove up and down the streets of the complex.

"There are sure a lot more security patrols out today. I wonder what is going on."

"I don't know, Farah. Maybe one of our mission operatives got into a confrontation, or was caught. But, I do know you were right when you said it would be impossible to get any closer to the tunnels."

"Look, there are several white-smocked scientists going toward one of the tunnel entrances."

"Okay, we'll have to launch the MAVs from here. I hope the underground facility isn't out of range, and that the mountain doesn't block our radio signals in the tunnel. And, I pray the tiny batteries will hold up for traveling to and from that far a distance." Zivah studied the lay of the land and plotted a route to the nearest tunnel entrance. Then they dropped back out of sight on the east side of the ridge. "Farah, put two MAVs on the ridge while I boot the notebook." Zivah launched and expertly guided the MAVs down the mountainside toward the tunnel entrance, using split screens on the notebook to navigate. "So far, so good."

"I will pray to Allah that our luck holds out, Zivah. I have a bad feeling about being too exposed."

"And I'll pray that Yahweh will not let us down. I'm going to direct the MAVs to follow that group into the tunnel now." The MAVs followed the last scientist through the security station and into the semi-darkness of the tunnel. "The audio is okay, but the video isn't too good in there. I'll switch to the night vision feature."

"That is much better. Now we can see and hear everything in the tunnel. This group is discussing the safety aspects of the storing UF6. But, I do not see anything stored in there."

"They might just be safety engineers. Look ahead . . . there's a bright light. I'll turn off the night vision before the light blinds the video cameras." The group of men walked into a huge room carved out deep in the mountain. About that time, the MAV transmittals on the notebook screen went snowy, and then totally black. "Oh, oh, we lost the radio signals. They're too deep in the mountain now, and I can't recall them."

"But, Zivah, what will happen to them?

"They will self-destruct if anyone tries to take them apart or operate them in any way. That underground room wasn't there when Iran let IAEA inspectors into the tunnel. I wish we could have seen what was in it, but at least we do have the last GPS coordinates before they stopped working." Zivah immediately uploaded the MAV data and site coordinates to her BlackBerry and transmitted them to Langley. "They're going to have to use Massive Ordnance Penetrators to take out this underground facility." She sent a text message to Langley and the team, "*lima two follow-up complete. hardened tunnel still good to go. cobra.*"

Langley replied, "*cobra. get out of there asap. hq.*"

"Farah, let's get going."

They hustled down the mountain as fast as the steep terrain would allow, avoiding the area where the leopard was still feasting. "We had better not drive directly back to Isfahan . . . just in case we were spotted."

"Good thinking, Farah. Where will this road take us if we head south?"

"It follows the Zayandeh River to the small village of Varzaneh and the Gavekhoni Marsh. There are camel trails leading out of the area to the east, and we can find our way back north to the Isfahan-Nain Highway somewhere along the way."

"Okay, you're the driver and I trust your judgment. *Booroh, booroh,* go, go!"

As Farah got up to top speed for the little Paykan, she looked in the rearview mirror and saw a military-type vehicle bearing down on them fast. "Zivah, we are in trouble! Look behind us."

Startled chickens went flying as they sped through Bajikabad mud village. Then occupants in the pursuit vehicle opened fire with full-automatic weapons. Zivah returned fire with her UZI. "Can't you go any faster? They're almost on top of us."

"I am going as fast as this old car will go. We are done for if they shoot out our tires."

As they entered Aminabad village, Zivah cried out, "Stop alongside that mud house on the left. We'll take cover inside."

Running into the house, Farah screamed in Persian at an old woman sitting on the dirt floor in front of a loom and weaving a carpet, "Get out of here, right now!" A younger woman was sitting on the floor and making yarn for the carpet weaver. She bolted out the doorway. The old woman, crippled with arthritis, slowly hobbled out behind her.

The pursuers screeched to a halt across the street and took cover behind their vehicle. Markings on the door indicated they were the elite Iranian Revolutionary Guards. However, a loud bellow in *Farsi* from their apparent leader sent shivers up and down the operatives' spines, "This is

VEVAK agent, Doctor Ali Kermani. I order you to put your weapons down and come out with your hands on top of your heads, now! If you do as I order, you will not be harmed."

"If you believe that, I can sell you the Golan Heights," Zivah whispered whimsically to Farah.

Zivah responded to Kermani's demand by setting her UZI's selector switch on single-shot, taking careful aim, and squeezing the trigger. One 9-millimeter slug hit the heart area of a Revolutionary Guard standing next to Kermani. Dropping his rifle, the guardsman went down for good while uttering a high-pitched squeal. Kermani and the other two guards crouched down behind their vehicle and wildly opened up on the mud house, pock marking the thick exterior wall. Several rounds from the guardsmen's 7.62-millimeter AK-47 rifles blew out the lone windowpane near the doorway.

Farah yelled, "What should I do? I am not trained on how to shoot my grandfather's submachine gun."

"Stay in the shadows, focus on the front sight, take careful aim at only one person, take a deep breath, let half of it out, and squeeze the trigger. The Sten doesn't have a single-shot selector switch, so hold the trigger back for one second to fire short, controlled bursts," Zivah replied calmly. "That way your weapon won't climb off the target area." Thoughts of Pat flashed through her mind, *Where are you when I need you, Patrick, my love?*

Farah positioned herself to shoot out of the window. Then she did exactly as Zivah instructed and immediately took out another guardsman with a burst of six or seven 9-millimeter rounds from her submachine gun. She exclaimed, loud enough for their enemies to hear her, "Praises to Allah! I got him, and he is in Hades now!"

Meanwhile, Zivah was exchanging gunfire through the doorway with Kermani and the remaining guardsman. She pointed to a clay water jug on the floor and motioned for Farah to toss it out through the window as she flipped the selector switch on her submachine gun back to single-shot mode. As the jug went flying, Zivah aimed in the direction of the two opponents. Kermani quickly stood up when he heard the sound of the jug crashing. He pointed and shot his ZOAF 9-millimeter pistol rapid-fire in that direction. Zivah took careful aim at his forehead and squeezed the trigger. The single round hit Kermani directly between the eyes and he immediately went down like a limp noodle. The infamous Doctor Ali Kermani finally met his Maker. Now it was Zivah's turn to exclaim, loud enough for the last guard to hear, "Praises to Yahweh! I eliminated one of the most evil men on earth, and he is also in *Sheol* now!"

The guardsman jumped into his vehicle to flee. However, the two operatives opened up with full-auto fire and he was killed instantly. The firefight ended as abruptly as it had started a few minutes earlier. "Take out the radio and tires too, Farah!"

"Will do. But first I will try to hit the petrol tank." The gas tank exploded after a few short bursts from her Sten. "Wow, what an invigorating, surreal experience. I am beginning to like this spy work!"

"Okay, good shooting! Let's get out of here, *right now*." On the way out of the hut, Zivah dropped 20,000 *toman* on a Persian carpet covered with 9-millmeter shell casings. She told Farah, "It's for the window pane and the water jug." Back in the car, she directed, "Continue heading south, in case they have backup on the way."

The pavement ended at the village of Varzaneh, where they drove down a dirt road to Gavekhoni Marsh. Farah explained, "This is where the Zayandeh River empties into swampland, which is a chain of freshwater marshes and

126

flood-plain wetlands bordering the Central Plateau desert on the east. We can not cross the marsh."

The Paykan created a large dust trail as they drove on a levee alongside the wetland. Then the sky filled with thousands of heavy-bodied gray-brown Greylag Geese with white under tails, green-necked Mallard Ducks, and Eurasian Wigeons with gray sides and russet face-markings. The birds were flushed by the engine noise and the dust created by their vehicle. Farah exclaimed, "This is the migration season . . . there must be millions of birds in the marsh!"

Finding a dirt road branching off to the east, just north of Gavekhoni Lake, Farah drove into the parched desert and headed toward Yazd. "We can not make it to the Isfahan-Nain Road from here. Besides, it is not safe to return to my villa."

"I agree. What do you have in mind?"

"I know where there is an Iranian People's Mujahedeen safe house across the desert in Yazd. I think they will take us in."

"Good thinking, Farah. Let's go there. Logan, one of our mission operatives, is hiding somewhere in that area, so maybe the Mujahedeen will know something about him."

The two women discussed their love life as they crossed the arid, ocher-hued salt desert region, "You know I have an ache in my heart for Patrick. I sure wish he was here now," Zivah expressed. "I have erotic thoughts about him all the time. I even thought about him in the middle of the firefight!"

"That sounds normal to me, my dear friend. I felt that way when I was younger. But, Persian men are no longer attractive to me. Perhaps because of their male dominance attitude."

"I don't blame you one bit, Farah. But, someday you will meet the right man."

"I certainly hope so! I yearn to be married and have children." After crossing the desert, they drove through the village of Nasrabad nestled between rolling tan-hued hills rounded by centuries of erosion. Then Farah followed a gravel road to the Taft Highway and headed east. She exclaimed, "I am sure glad we are back on a paved road. The bouncing around on that dusty track was starting to get to me!"

"Me too! I'm covered with desert dust from head to toe. Let's make up for lost time."

Farah floor-boarded the little Paykan. They drove through the towns of Fazabad and Taft, and then past an underground water reservoir with six wind funnel cooling towers. Entering Yazd, she turned right on Sadoqi Farokhi and they went past a Zoroastrian fire temple. At the central square, she turned right on Hasan Dashti, and then left into a small *kuche* where they stopped behind a two-story apartment building. "This is it. I hope we do not need a password to get in."

After ringing the rear gate bell, a booming male voice commanded over the intercom, "Who are you?" in *Farsi*.

Farah responded, "Please help us! The Revolutionary Guards and VEVAK are after us. Let us in, *Aga*, and we will tell you our story."

"So, you are the ones they are talking about on NIRT News!"

Looking up, Zivah spotted a rifle barrel pointing at them from a second story window. She replied, "Yes, yes. We are in desperate need of your help."

The rifle barrel disappeared as the gate latch buzzed, and the intercom voice said, "Come in. We have one of your mission team members here."

As they entered the courtyard and walked toward the door, Zivah commented, "That must be Logan."

Farah cautioned, "Do not let the Mujahedeen know you are Israeli. If they ask, tell them you are Turkish."

Upstairs, Logan ran out into the hallway and yelled, "Zivah! I thought they might have caught you two. You know, you are both on the news, although they don't know who you are." Bowing to the two female operatives, he continued, "You're heroes to some, for slaying Doctor Ali Kermani. But, you're wanted terrorists by the government."

While giving Logan a long hug, Zivah said, "So we heard. I'm glad you're safe too." She immediately sent a text message to Langley and the team with her BlackBerry, "*cobra safe with adder at undisclosed location. get coordinates from gps signal.*"

Langley replied, "*cobra. it's done. get out of country. good luck. hq.*"

Logan then told Zivah about the demise of Farhad.

The Mujahedeen leader, Abbas, gave Zivah and Farah small glasses of hot *chahee* and a bowl of sugar cubes. The two women put a sugar cube between their teeth and sipped their tea through the cubes. After they took a few sips, he said in broken English, "We get you to Zahedan, across *Dasht-e-Lut*. Jundallah Sunnis fight Iranian government there, and they help you cross border to Afghanistan. Then you find American and British troops looking for al-Qaeda and Taliban. They help you."

"That sounds like a good plan to me," Zivah stated. "Let's get out of Persia before the fireworks start."

Logan chimed in, "Indeed. I know that desert very well, and I agree. The sooner we leave, the better chance we will have of making it out of Iran alive."

Farah exclaimed, "What about me? I do not want to go to Afghanistan, and it is too dangerous to go back to Isfahan right now."

Abbas spoke up, "You stay here until they stop looking. We take you home when it safe."

Zivah gave Farah a long, loving hug and kissed her on both of her dusty cheeks. "Thank you for helping us during this important mission, and for putting your life in danger." She handed Farah an envelope and continued, "Take this $5,000 U.S. as payment for your brave service, and make a good life for you and your mother. *Khoda Hafez!*"

Farah responded with tears in her eyes, "*Khoda Hafez* my dear, dear Zivah!"

Abbas anxiously ordered, "We leave now. Travel desert in darkness."

CHAPTER EIGHT: EXTRACTIONS

Day Seven: Viper Leader, Copperhead, Asp

Pat, Alev, and Ari were up an hour before daybreak. Nader's *khanom*, Geeso, provided a light breakfast of *nan-e-bahr-bahr-ee*, fresh butter, oranges, and hot Caspian *chahee*. Then Pat directed, "Time to go."

Alev handed the Samand keys to her cousin, Nader, and commented, "Keep the vehicle as a gift of our appreciation for your hospitality and safe haven. You must have it painted a different color and change the license plates, in case the authorities have a description of the vehicle from my confrontations at Chalus and on the Astara-Tabriz Highway." She then put on a headscarf. The three operatives said goodbye to the couple and were on their way before the sun rose over the eastern hills.

As Ari drove the Land Rover out of town, they went past a 14th century citadel, and then the 12-sided tomb of Mongol dynasty ruler, Mahmud Ghazan. They headed northwest at high speed on the Khoy Highway. After several miles, Pat directed, "Turn left on this side road coming up. It's a less-traveled route, and it will parallel the old Iran-Turkey railroad tracks."

Now heading west, Ari stated, "We can't make very good time on this narrow, twisting road."

"I know, but it's a lot safer than taking a chance on being stopped by patrols on the main highway," Pat responded. They went through Shabestar, then the port village of Sharaf Khane on the north shore of Lake Urmia. After the operatives went through the town of Sharpur, they entered the Urmia-Sharpur Highway.

While they were heading south toward Urmia, the occupants of an oncoming military vehicle slowed down and eyed them. "Don't look at them. Look straight ahead," Pat warned. "Ari, watch them in the rearview mirror. We'll make a run for it if they turn around." Luckily, Alev had her hair covered with a scarf.

A minute or so later, Ari said, "It looks like they're continuing north."

"Whew, that was another close one . . . I was getting ready for a firefight! My heart is beating a hundred kilometers an hour," Alev gasped. She put her hand on her left breast and remarked, with an impish grin, "Here, Patrick, feel my heart racing."

"Thanks, but no thanks. This isn't the time for your sexual antics, Alev."

Ari merely grinned.

Approaching the large city of Urmia, Pat changed the topic and volunteered, "This town and lake were called Rezaiyeh when I was here before. The new regime must have changed it after the revolution. Ari, as we get into the north side of town, take the Qods Expressway to the west. Turn right at the end of the expressway. It may not be signed as such, but that road will take us to the border at Sero. Esendere, Turkey is just across the frontier."

"Then I'll be back home," Alev gleefully shouted as she wiggled her torso. She continued, "Rezaiyeh is located on the large, fertile Urmia Plain. It was seized and occupied by Turkey many times in the past. We should have just kept it!"

Ari followed Pat's driving instructions. Heading northwest, they went past cultivated fields, green pastures, and lush fruit orchards. After the road curved sharply to the left, they drove through bare, rolling foothills. Higher in the

132

mountains, the trio neared the town of Sero. It took about four hours to drive the 175 miles from Tabriz.

"We better find a way to avoid the border check station. They might be looking for us," Alev suggested.

"I can use the four-wheel drive feature to maneuver across there to the border," Ari interjected as he pointed at a bare hill.

"Or, we can drive along the north shore of the Sero River," Pat said. "There are some trees and other foliage in the riparian hollow that will give us at least some cover."

"That sounds good to me," Ari replied.

"Me too," Alev agreed. Ari put the Land Rover in four-wheel drive and drove slowly down a steep embankment to the stream. Creeping along over large, smooth river rocks and around logs on the riverbank was tedious and seemed to take forever. Running out of patience so close to her homeland, Alev finally shouted, "I've had it. I would rather shoot my way through the border check station and crash through the barricade into Turkey!"

"Relax, Alev, relax," Pat soothed her. "We're almost there, and this isn't the time to panic!"

Approaching the frontier, Ari shouted, "There's multiple strands of barbed wire stretched across the river and both shores. What do we do now?"

Pat replied, "Get the wire cutters out of the tool box. I'll cut our way through. Let's make it fast because I'm sure this area is heavily patrolled." As Pat was about to cut the last strand of barbed wire, they heard a vehicle stop at the top of the south embankment. "Ready your UZIs. We're in for it!" The three operatives flicked off the safeties and set the selector switches to full-auto on their submachine guns.

Shouts in *Farsi*, coming from someone hidden behind a clump of bushes using a megaphone, echoed down the hollow, "This is the Islamic Republic of Iran Border Patrol. Stop where you are, put down your weapons, and place your hands on top of your heads or we will shoot!"

Pat instructed his team, in a low voice, "Do as they ordered, but be ready to double-tap them with your pistols when they approach." The operatives carefully placed their UZIs on the ground and put their hands on top of their heads.

As three heavily armed border patrol agents scrambled down the steep embankment across the 30-foot-wide river, Pat uttered, "I'll take the one on the right."

"I'll take the middle one," Ari whispered.

"I've got the one on the left," Alev said softly.

As the last border patrol agent's boots landed on the rocky shore, Pat shouted, "Now!" The operatives drew their pistols and fired simultaneously. All of them hit their respective targets with two rounds to the chest and one round in the forehead. The three Iranian agents went down immediately.

"More dirty camels bite the dust!" Alev screamed.

The Iranian with the megaphone yelled in *Farsi* "Fire, fire, fire!" The border patrol agents on top of the embankment opened up with full-automatic weapons.

Ari and Alev returned fire with their UZIs as Pat raced for the Land Rover and jumped into the driver's seat. "Get in!" he hollered while firing his UZI one-handed in the direction of the border patrol's shots. Ari and Alev jumped head first into the backseat of the Land Rover and Pat crashed the vehicle through the last strand of barbed wire and onto Turkish soil.

However, the Iranians continued to fire at the fleeing operatives after they crossed the frontier, and one of their rounds hit Ari in the left calf. He screamed, "I'm hit!"

Republic of Turkey Border Patrol agents, hearing the gunfire from their border check station, arrived and shot their weapons up in the air. Then a spokesman with a megaphone ordered in Persian, "Iranian Border Patrol, cease fire or we will shoot to kill!"

The Iranians immediately stopped shooting and drove off. The Turks then focused on the three mission operatives. The spokesman ordered them in Turkish, "Stop and get out of the vehicle, now! You three put your hands up, and keep them up until we determine what is going on."

Alev replied, "*Selam, efendi*. My name is Alev Barak and I am an OHD agent."

The Turk with the megaphone told his agents to lower their weapons. Then he ordered, "Drive your vehicle up the embankment."

Pat drove up to where the Turks were waiting and stopped. Alev suggested softly, "Let me do the talking."

As the border patrol agents walked up to Land Rover, the spokesman grinned widely and said, "We have been waiting for you, Agent Barak. Your superiors in Ankara notified all three Turkey-Iran border crossing stations that you may be coming through today. Welcome back to Turkey."

Alev sighed in relief, and then tended to Ari's wound. "It's just a flesh wound, my friend, and the blood is starting to congeal."

"But it hurts like Hades!" Ari complained.

Alev retorted, "Do you want me to kiss it?" All three of the operatives broke out in uncontrollable laughter. The Turks just stared in bewilderment at the trio.

Alev called OHD Headquarters from the Border Patrol Station and asked for a plane to pick them up at Yuksekova Airport. The Commandant then ordered one of his agents to drive the team to Yuksekova. Alev fluttered her eyelashes at him. He smiled and nodded, as if they may have known each other sometime in the past.

Meanwhile, Pat sent a text message to Langley and the rest of the team, *"viper leader, copperhead, asp safely out of country. viper leader."*

Langley replied, *"viper leader. great. welcome back. hq."*

The border patrol agent drove the trio of operatives down the mountain on the twisty Yuksekova-Esendere Highway. They traveled alongside the fast-flowing Esendere River and past bright green hillsides covered with colorful blue and yellow wildflowers. Alev exclaimed, "It's wonderful to be back home! Isn't this beautiful countryside?"

"Yes, and it's great to be out of Persia," Pat replied.

Ari chimed in, "I agree, Alev. This *is* beautiful, just like you!"

With a twinkle in her eyes. Alev smiled knowingly at Ari.

Further down the mountain, still following the river, they went near the villages of Akpinar and Kisikli. The highway was heavily patrolled by Turkish Army troops. They were stopped at an army checkpoint and the border patrol agent explained who his passengers were and where he was taking them. A sergeant waved them through the roadblock as he warned, "This is Turkish Kurdistan territory, so be watchful for Kurd insurgents." He then gave Alev a big grin and a wink. Alev smiled and winked back.

She must have known the sergeant sometime in the past, like the border patrol commandant, Pat contemplated.

Dropping down to a lower elevation, they passed by verdant farmlands and orchards filled with ripe fruit. Entering Yuksekova, Ari commented, "I passed through here with Sadar last week." It was twenty-four miles from Esendere and the trip took about an hour.

There was an OHD Learjet waiting for them at the airport. After boarding, Alev sat next to Pat, even though there was enough room to spread out comfortably with just the three operatives in the passenger cabin. The plane lifted off and climbed fast and high to clear the surrounding mountain peaks. Once above the mountain range, the trio had a panoramic view of Lake Van to the north and majestic snow-capped Mount Ararat in the background.

Alev leaned over Pat to look out the window and rubbed her voluptuous breasts against his muscular upper arm, just as Zivah did on the flight from Istanbul to Van the week before. Pat continued to gaze out the window. Not getting a response from him, Alev sat back in her seat and pouted for a while. However, not one to give up, she rubbed her hand along Pat's inner thigh as they flew over the eastern Anatolia mountains. "Patrick, we can get adjoining rooms at the hotel in Ankara tonight," she cooed amorously, all the while thinking, *If only Zivah could see me now!*

Pat responded with a curt, "Alev, we went through this before. You're over sexed. Just let it be." Again, she sat back in her seat and pouted, this time with a grimace on her face.

Ari, observing Alev's antics and Pat's rebuffs, smiled, chuckled to himself and peered out the window.

Changing the subject, Pat asked Alev, "What is that lake and dam to the north?"

"That's Keban Dam and Lake Keban, which is fed by the Euphrates River," she replied peevishly while still frowning. "It's Turkey's third largest lake." Then she pondered, *Am I merely his tour guide now?*

Still peering out the window a few moments later, Ari called out, "Look! What a spectacular view of sprawling

Ankara! I can see green parks, industrial area smoke stacks, residential neighborhoods, and huge palaces."

Alev forgot about her annoyance with Pat and said, "That's my nation's capital, and it's the second largest city in Turkey, after Istanbul. Did you know that Ankara has a history dating back to the Bronze Age?" Pat and Ari nodded in acknowledgement.

About that time, the pilot circled once and landed at Esenboga Airport outside of the city, ending the 650-mile flight. An OHD limo was waiting for the trio as they disembarked. During the drive to the city center, they went past the Citadel of Ankara built high on a hill by King Midas. "Old Ankara is inside the citadel walls. It's a nice place to enjoy fine Turkish cuisine and watch curvaceous belly dancers perform," Alev volunteered as she wiggled her hips and breasts provocatively.

"I'd like to see Old Ankara, if we have the time," Pat remarked.

"I'll show both of you the sights in the Old City," Alev responded. They continued toward the hotel and went past the Temple of Augustus. Again, Alev offered, "This ancient temple was built in the year 10 A.D."

"What is that beautiful mosque next to the temple?" Ari inquired.

"That's the Haci Bayram Mosque." *Maybe I really am their tour guide,* she mused.

They soon arrived at the Ankara Hilton Hotel on Ataturk Boulevard. The 21-mile trip from the airport took about 35 minutes, and the total distance they traveled from Tabriz that day was 870 miles.

After checking in, Pat sent Langley and the rest of the team a text message, *"viper leader, copperhead, asp safe at location mike. viper leader."*

Langley replied, *"viper leader. adder and cobra arriving soon. hq."*

Pat took a long, well-needed hot shower. Then he met Alev and Ari for drinks at the Hilton's Lotus Bar. After unwinding, Pat announced, "Zivah and Logan just texted me. They should be here soon. Let's meet them in front of the hotel."

Day Five continued: Adder, Cobra

Zivah covered her hair with a scarf. Then she, Logan, and the Mujahedeen leader, Abbas, got into a black, dust covered Mercedes-Benz sports utility vehicle and drove south on Hasan Dashti Avenue. The early evening quietness was broken by a *muezzin's* enchanting call to prayer emitting from a minaret at a neighborhood Yazd mosque. The trio headed southeast out of town on the Yazd-Kerman Highway.

Shams village was nearly dark, with just dim lights shining from a few mud hut windows as they drove through at high speed. Entering the town of Rafsandjan, Abbas cautioned, "You look for police and military." He emphasized his command by holding a hand at his brow, as if shading his eyes from bright sunlight to see better, and continued, "They look for you."

Both operatives smiled at his comical gesture.

Further down the road, as they were about to enter the village of Kabutarkhan, Zivah asked, "What variety of trees are those shimmering in the soft glow of the moonlight?"

"Pistachio nuts," Abbas replied gruffly, obviously not wanting to be involved in small talk.

"Zivah, me lady, this region, particularly between Rafsandjan and Kerman, grows most of the pistachios in

Persia. They are the best in the world, and I can eat them by the bagful," Logan offered.

The highway skirted the southern edge of the *Dasht-e-Lut* wilderness as they approached Kerman. The clay brick city was alive with lights, and people walked up and down the avenues as the trio drove down Doctor Shari'ati Boulevard. "Keep head covered, woman," Abbas cautioned Zivah.

Azadi Square was teeming with young men and women as they drove past the gathering place. Some of them were holding hands, and this prompted Logan to comment, "It looks like the young people are enjoying the pleasant evening."

Abbas responded, "Yes. But government *mullahs* do not like mixed man and woman activity in public."

Zivah interjected, "I understand that a woman in the company of the opposite sex, other than her immediate family and her spouse, is guilty of a crime punishable by the whip or even prison!" Abbas merely nodded an affirmative.

Logan commented, "Var Bazaar is also busy. It looks like late evening shoppers bargaining for carpets and gold jewelry." After going by the Islamic Azad University campus, and the 12th century Mountain of Stone dome, they headed southeast on the Kerman-Zahedan Highway.

Passing over a range of desolate mountains, the road dropped down into the shifting golden sand dunes and barren undulating hills of the vast *Dasht-e-Lut*. The radiance of moonbeams danced on 1,000-foot tall dunes that looked similar to the Kelso Dunes in California's Mojave Desert. Zivah cried out, "That is certainly an eerie scene!"

Logan replied, "It most certainly is, me lass." They sped through the darkened villages of Mahan and Neybid and soon approached Bam. Logan volunteered, "This city is located at the crossroads of important ancient trade routes, and the buildings are made with mud and clay brick. Essentially, the oasis was created in the parched desert environment with the construction of *qanats*. The hand-dug underground canals bring precious water from the distant mountains."

"Bam destroyed by earthquake several years ago. 26,000 people die," Abbas offered.

"Yes, I remember that. It was on the news for weeks," Zivah replied.

Logan added, "It was a bloody 6.6 magnitude quake in 2003. I understand that Old Bam dates back to the 6th century BC, and it was totally ruined by the earthquake. Bam is the most representative example of a fortified town in Persia."

Further down the road, they entered the village of Narmshar. Then the highway headed northeast across flat, salt desert wasteland. Zivah dozed off a few times and dreamt about being with Pat. Meanwhile, they drove through the desolate village of Shurgaz in the middle of the night.

After traveling down a long, lonely stretch of desert highway, they reached Nosratabad village. Abbas declared, "We close to Zahedan now. Must watch for government troops. They seek Jundallah Sunnis that kill General Shooshtari and Chief Commander Mohsammadzaeh of the Iranian Revolutionary Guards."

The 450-mile trip across the desert from Yazd to Zahedan took nearly seven hours. While driving into the city center, they went past the darkened University of Zahedan and the Rasouli Bazaar. Abbas parked the SUV in the courtyard of Makki Mosque at 0300 hours. Getting out of the vehicle, he said, "This greatest mosque of Sunnites in Persia. You wait." Then he disappeared into the shadows.

Zivah exclaimed, "I don't like this. It's too dark and quiet."

"I'm sure we're okay. However, be prepared for anything."

Zivah sent Langley and the rest of the team a text message, "*cobra and adder relocated. get coordinates from gps signal. cobra.*"

Langley replied, "*cobra. got it. hq.*"

Both operatives readied their UZIs in case they were set up for an ambush. A few minutes later, Abbas returned with a gray-bearded, sleepy-eyed cleric wearing a turban. After cursory introductions by Abbas, the cleric said, in perfect British English, "I am Abd, the leader of the Sunni militant group, Jundallah of Iran. We are also called the People's Resistance Movement of Iran. Because you fight against the oppressive Iranian government, Jundallah will help you as brothers and sisters in arms." He motioned toward Abbas and continued, "Just like the Iranian People's Mujahedeen."

Reassured, Zivah and Logan replied "*Merci, Aga.*"

Then Zivah addressed the cleric, "I understand that you are fighting for the same rights that the Shia's have in Persia."

"You are absolutely correct, young lady. We are fighting the hard-line Shia government for the Allah-given rights of the Sunni Islam sect, as well as for the rights of Iran's Baloch tribe in this region."

Zivah and Logan told Abbas they appreciated his help. After saluting the two operatives, the Mujahedeen leader headed back toward Yazd.

Motioning toward the mosque, Abd directed the operatives, "Follow me. You must rest for your arduous and perilous forthcoming journey."

Feeling somewhat secure inside the mosque grounds, Zivah and Logan fell into deep, well deserved sleeps.

Day Six: Adder, Cobra

Abd woke up Logan and Zivah about four hours later with the announcement, "It is a long trek. You should bathe and eat before your departure." An hour later, he led them to a Mercedes-Benz minibus parked in the courtyard. Heavily armed escorts, five men and a woman, were already on the bus. "I will go to the border near Hormak with you to ensure safe passage that far. My soldiers will then take you into Afghanistan and help you find Western coalition troops."

There were violent demonstrations in the streets of Zahedan, especially around the university and the bazaar. Zivah asked, "Abd, what in the world is going on here?"

"This is a continuation of the earlier demonstrations over the disputed re-election of the President, as well as a show of sorrow over the death of a high-ranking leader and dissident in our nation's religious establishment. We must avoid the area." Abd ordered the driver to turn around and directed him to take an alternate route.

"Look, those blokes are shooting into the crowd," Logan hollered as the driver made a u-turn on the boulevard.

"Yes, that is the Basiji Militia, and they will not hesitate to use deadly force against anti-government protesters," Abd replied. "They are more evil than the Iranian Revolutionary Guards that they report directly to."

Zivah chimed in, "It looks like the protesters are in hand-to-hand combat with the government forces . . . they're torching vehicles."

Abd told the driver, "*Booroh, booroh,* Seyyed!" The driver heeded his leader's hurry up command and floorboarded the minibus. They left Zahedan and drove due north. The highway went past the pointed intersection of the Pakistan-Afghanistan-Iran borders. It was just a short distance more to Hormak village.

Leaving the paved road, Seyyed headed straight east on a dirt track from Hormak to the Afghanistan frontier. He stopped at an international boundary marker and Abd disembarked while saying, "Be aware, you may encounter Iranian intelligence agents transferring money to the Taliban insurgents that they support. For your safety, try to avoid them. Good luck, my friends. May Allah be with you."

Zivah and Logan thanked him. Then Abd got into a waiting car and headed back to Zahedan. The armed escorts spoke Yazdi, a Persian dialect that Zivah did not quite understand. However, Logan was somewhat familiar with the language and he could communicate with them. Seyyed crossed the unguarded frontier into Nimruz Province in the Islamic Emirate of Afghanistan. He then drove into the huge *Dasht-e-Margo* wilderness.

Logan remarked, "Zivah, I'll let Langley and the team know we've left Iran. They can determine our location and Langley will notify U.N. coalition troops that we're in Afghanistan."

"Excellent idea."

He then sent the text message, "*adder and cobra safely out of country. get coordinates from gps signal. adder.*"

Langley replied, "*adder. it's done. be careful. hq.*"

While riding over rolling hills and sand masses in the wilderness, Mitra, the female escort and apparent leader said, in Yazdi, "This is a little-known smuggler's route. It should keep us away from the Taliban until we reach Helmand Province."

144

Logan nodded and translated her message for Zivah. The track went along the north side of the huge Zereh Depression and south of the Helmand River basin.

The driver stopped on the outskirts of Rudbar village on the river. Several Afghani villagers walked up to the minibus, spoke Yazdi to the Jundallah soldiers, and then they exchanged blanket-covered bundles. Mitra told Logan, "We bartered illicit goods with our Sunni brothers."

Logan responded, "Of course, that is none of our business."

"Was it opium . . . arms . . . alcohol?" Zivah inquired.

Logan shrugged his shoulders and replied, "Possibly. I didn't ask."

They continued easterly on the dirt track and were soon in a zero-visibility sandstorm. Seyyed stopped the minibus, and fifty to sixty-mile-an-hour winds hit the vehicle and sandblasted it.

Coughing from fine dust in the vehicle, Zivah exclaimed, "I'm sure glad we aren't out in this on foot!" as the minibus rocked back and forth. The storm blew over a half-hour later, and the scorching hot sun returned, exposing pitted windows and large areas of paint stripped off the vehicle.

Seyyed continued east across the desert. It was not long before they were amid a sea of bright orange poppy fields waving in the breeze of southern Helmand Province. Mitra cautioned, "Now we look out for the Taliban. They control the province, and the opium money derived from poppies supports their war efforts." Pointing south, she continued, "Al-Qaeda may also be in this region because it is so close to the mountains in Pakistan. They are Sunnis, but they are *not* our brothers in arms."

Logan replied, "I understand," and conveyed the warning to Zivah. The distant mountains on the Pakistan

145

frontier looked purplish, and the alluvial plains at their base appeared to be golden sand spotted with large clumps of vegetation.

South of Marjah, they spotted a British patrol convoy approaching in the distance. The minibus driver attached a white flag to the top of his vehicle's radio antenna. Then the convoy stopped and the British troops took cover behind their vehicles. Seyyed proceeded slowly toward the convoy and stopped immediately when a voice commanded over a megaphone, "This is Captain Lord of the British Army. Halt and identify yourself."

Logan ordered, in Yazdi and then in English, "Everyone stay in the vehicle. I will take care of this." Leaving his weapons on the minibus, he exited with his hands on top of his head. Then he hollered, "I'm Logan Johnson, MI6 agent. I have Zivah Benjamin, a MOSSAD agent, with me. We were on a mission in Iran. You can verify this with your headquarters staff. They should be expecting us, and we need to get to Kandahar Airbase as soon as possible." Pointing back at the minibus, he added, "Our escorts are comrades that brought us to you. Please allow them to return to Iran now."

Logan heard someone in the convoy using a tactical radio for several minutes. Captain Lord finally replied over the megaphone, "Your story is confirmed. You and Agent Benjamin come forward with your weapons held high. The Iranians are free to return to their homeland."

Logan thanked the Jundallah escorts and they departed. He and Zivah walked over to the British convoy with their UZIs and pistols held over their heads. They were greeted by the troops with cheers, applause, and given large sips of rum. Captain Lord then commanded, "Load up. Let's make sure these heroes get to Kandahar."

While the convoy drove through a huge poppy field below a low ridge, Zivah pointed at a figure on the ridgeline and yelled, "We've got company!" Just then, a rocket launched from the hill took out the convoy's point vehicle. Captain Lord hollered over his radio, "Incoming! Disperse, disperse, it's the Taliban. Return fire at will!"

As the British vehicles spread out into the field, the troops began returning fire. Zivah and Logan fired their UZIs toward the hill, but the enemy was just out of effective range for their 9-millimeter submachine gun rounds. Zivah yelled, "Aim high, Logan, aim high. Maybe some of our rounds will hit the insurgents."

The British convoy was being peppered with rocket-propelled grenades and AK-47 rounds when a commanding voice came over their tactical radios, "This is Lieutenant Freeman, U.S. Marine Corps. We're approaching from your rear and will give you fire support."

"This is Captain Lord, British Expeditionary Forces. Come on in lieutenant. Glad you're here. The enemy is on the ridge directly in front of us."

The Marines zeroed-in on the ridgeline and bombarded it with devastating 120-millimeter rifled mortar rounds, .50-caliber M2 heavy machinegun fire, and a 25-millimeter M242 Bushmaster chain gun. The Brits and Marines took out the aggressors and the firefight soon ended. Within a few minutes, Lieutenant Freeman drove up and Captain Lord introduced himself and the two operatives.

Logan addressed Freeman, "Lieutenant, we need to get to Kandahar Airbase ASAP. Can you have a helicopter pick us up?"

"Can do, sir," Freeman replied. "I'll radio in to have you picked up right here, and you'll be in Kandahar *tout de suite*."

Meanwhile, Captain Lord asked his lieutenants for casualty reports. They reported four British soldiers dead and six wounded. He then ordered his troops to set the poppy field afire.

"There goes some of the funding for the Taliban," Zivah expressed with glee.

A CH-53E Super Stallion chopper arrived within an hour, and the Marines popped yellow smoke grenades to indicate a safe landing zone away from the burning poppy field. The Marine pilot landed, creating a huge dust cloud. Everyone on the ground covered their faces to protect against the biting sand hitting them. Logan yelled, "This is as bad as a bloody sandstorm!"

Lieutenant Freeman and Captain Lord spoke to the Super Stallion crew and the operatives were allowed to board. After brief introductions to the two pilots and three gunners, the chopper lifted off and headed northeast. When they were airborne, one of the pilots announced over the intercom, "We have orders to avoid the Marjah area because of a fierce battle with the Taliban there. The insurgents also hold the ground to the west of town. However, our radar picked up a sandstorm coming in from the east of Marjah. Super Stallions don't do well in sandstorms, so it's going to be dicey squeezing in between the town and the sandstorm."

Addressing Logan, Zivah uttered, with a wry smile, "After what we've been through, what's new?"

Logan merely chuckled aloud. The pilot expertly guided his chopper up a narrow slot between Marjah and the approaching dark, ominous-looking sandstorm, and they barely missed being hit by the storm.

The flight to the NATO Kandahar Airbase didn't take long, and they soon were landing in front of the terminal building. As a High-mobility Multipurpose Wheeled Vehicle pulled up to the chopper, the pilot announced,

"They're expecting you. Good luck, and enjoy your short stay at Candy Bar."

Zivah and Logan responded, with a heart-felt, "Thank you."

Zivah added, "Absolutely great flying, Pilot!"

NATO fighter jets screamed overhead, and combat helicopters hovered for landing sites, as the operatives jumped into the waiting Humvee. That long day, the distance traveled from Zahedan to Kandahar was approximately 800 miles.

CIA and MI6 agents debriefed the operatives at a secure building. After an hour of intense questioning, the interviewers said they would send their findings to their respective headquarters. Zivah and Logan were escorted to a NATO officers' mess for a welcome hot meal. Then the U.S. Air Force put them up in rooms at the officers' billets. They slept like babies throughout the night.

Day Seven continued: Adder, Cobra

The operatives were up early and ate a hearty breakfast in the officers' mess. Then they boarded a U.S. Air Force C-130J Hercules transport plane heading for Baghdad, Iraq. After getting settled in their seats, Zivah sent Langley and the rest of the team a text message, "*wheels going up. arriving balad today. cobra and adder.*"

Langley replied, "*cobra and adder. meet ohd jet at balad. hq.*"

The plane lifted off and, as they reached cruising altitude, two Reaper drones heading in the direction of Helmand Province whizzed past about a quarter mile from them. "Look at the unmanned drones. What a sight," exclaimed Logan. "The Taliban and al-Qaeda are sure in for it today."

"Did you know that Israel now has a fleet of Heron TP drones?" Zivah replied.

"I heard that from our Intel people. You'll be ready if the Arabs or Iranians attack your homeland."

"That we will, Logan. That we will. You know that Iran recently unveiled a long-range unmanned bomber, the Karrar. It can carry four cruise missiles, and has a range of 620 miles. That puts Tel Aviv almost within its range if the drone is launched from near the Iraq border."

"That's way too bloody close for comfort. However, I understand that the Herons can also reach Tehran."

"They can, and the entire Persian Gulf region is well within their range," Zivah enthusiastically replied.

The pilot headed due south, entered the Islamic Republic of Pakistan airspace, and continued to the Gulf of Oman. Then she changed course and flew west, crossing over the United Arab Emirates Peninsula to avoid the Strait of Hormuz and potential guided missiles launched from Iran. Changing course again, she headed northwest up the Persian Gulf, flew over Kuwait, and entered Iraqi airspace and the Biblical Cradle of Civilization region.

"I can see Korramshahr across the peninsula at the confluence of the Shatt al-Arab and the Karun River. That's where I entered Iran when we were inserted last week," Logan stated.

Zivah nodded in acknowledgement. The pilot flew up the Euphrates River delta and landed at Balad U.S. Air Force Base near Baghdad. Zivah told Logan, "My chopper landed here to refuel the day I was inserted near Isfahan."

A Turkish OHD Learjet was waiting for them at the airfield and the operatives boarded it after thanking the Hercules crew for the ride. The pilot took off, headed north, and followed an oil pipeline just west of the Tigris River. They could see sprawling Mosul to the east, and the Syrian frontier to the west. The plane soon approached an Iraqi oilfield at the intersection of the Iraq-Syria-Turkey borders. After flying over Zakhu, Iraq, they entered Turkish airspace. Then the pilot set a course to the northwest and headed directly toward Ankara.

"Look at beautiful, snow-capped Mount Ararat," Zivah squealed in delight.

"You know, this must be at least the tenth time I've had an aerial view of that spectacular sight. I would never tire of looking at the legendary Biblical mount."

They were soon landing at Esenboga Airport, and an OHD limousine was waiting for them as they disembarked. The air distance traveled from Kandahar to Ankara was close to 3,000 miles.

Logan sent Langley and Pat a text message, "*adder and cobra safe at location mike. hotel eta approx 30 minutes. adder and cobra.*"

Langley replied, "*adder and cobra. good news. welcome back. hq.*"

"I'm anxious about seeing Patrick. There are butterflies in my stomach," Zivah confided in Logan during the ride to the Ankara Hilton Hotel.

"I know he likes you as much as you like him, Zivah. I wouldn't worry. In fact, if I didn't realize that, I would have made a play for you during the past few days. Age difference be damned . . . you are a very beautiful woman."

Zivah blushed and smiled sweetly, then squeezed his hand as she murmured, "Thank you, dear friend. Thank you." She was over her anxiety by the time they reached the hotel.

Pat, Ari, and Alev were waiting in front of the Hilton when the limo drove up. They approached to greet their comrades as the driver opened the door. Amid handshakes, hugs, and kisses, Pat whispered in Zivah's ear, "I sure missed you!"

Her bright white teeth and dark brown eyes sparkled as she smiled widely. Then she whispered demurely in Pat's ear, "I'm all yours tonight, My Love."

Pat grinned from ear to ear and replied, "And, I'm all yours, My Charming Zivah." Then he addressed her and Logan, "You two check-in and freshen up. We'll all dine together this evening at the Greenhouse Restaurant in the hotel." He sent a text message to Langley, *"entire team at location mike. mission complete. viper leader."*

Langley replied, *"viper leader. congratulations for a job well done. hq."*

The five operatives enjoyed a typical Turkish dinner of lamb stew and *dolmas*. They topped of the fine meal with *baklava* and strong Turkish coffee served in demitasse cups. While holding Zivah's hand at the table, Pat noticed Alev flirting with Ari, the waiter, and any male that happened to walk by their table. *Alev's ignoring me now . . . I guess she's really peeved at me, or trying to make me jealous*, Pat reasoned. After dinner, he announced, "Our HQ officers will be here in the morning. We'll meet in the Ararat Conference Room for a debriefing at 0800 hours sharp."

Logan told Pat, "I'll be there. Ta ta. I'm going to Old Ankara now and watch the sexy belly dancers perform."

"Don't be late for the meeting in the morning," Pat cautioned. "By the way, I was just informed that my Tehran contact, Hossein, and his wife were given political asylum in the U.S."

Walking back to their rooms, with his arm around Zivah's tiny waist, Pat wondered, *Will Alev make another pass at me now?* The thought was short-lived. Pat turned around to say good night just as Ari followed Alev into her room and quietly closed the door. "Well, I guess that proves Ari isn't gay," he expressed to Zivah as they entered her room.

She winked knowingly.

CHAPTER NINE: ANKARA

Day Eight: Viper Leader, Copperhead, Asp, Adder, Cobra

After a well-needed night of relaxation, the operatives met for breakfast at the Ankara Hilton's Greenhouse Restaurant. Pat cautioned, "No mission talk until we're in the conference room. It's been checked for bugs and it's clean."

They savored warm *baklava*, strong Turkish coffee, fresh fruit, and chilled prickly pear nectar to start the day. Mimicking Pat on the OHD jet the previous week, Alev exclaimed, "Ah! Food for a Goddess!" as she reached toward the Heavens. The other four team members chuckled at her animated antics.

Pat and Zivah, as well as Ari and Alev, were holding hands at the breakfast table. This prompted Logan to comment, "Here is a wonderful illustration of the meeting of East and West . . . Christian and Jew . . . Jew and Muslim," as he waved toward the two moonstruck couples. All four of them blushed and smiled as he continued, with a wide grin, "I too had a delightful Occidental and Oriental encounter with a belly dancer last night, and I did my part to further international relations." They all broke out into uncontrollable laughter, thus releasing the tensions of the harrowing events of their mission in Iran during the past week. Nearby restaurant patrons stared at them and shook their heads in disbelief.

One special agent from each of the four represented agencies, appearing as stone-faced as Buckingham Palace sentries, guarded the door to the Ararat Conference Room. However, they did nod greetings to the five operatives as they entered. They nodded back. Alev smiled and coyly blew a kiss at the OHD agent. He smiled back and winked at her. Pat thought, *Aha, another one of Alev's many conquests!*

Top echelon officers from the CIA, OHD, MOSSAD, and MI6 were waiting for them as they entered the conference room. The headquarters staff stood up and applauded. The CIA's Chief Special Agent, Retired Colonel Nathan Connery, announced, "All five of you are heroes, and we're proud of you!" Then the officers shook their hands while introducing themselves.

As he shook Pat's hand, Colonel Connery said warmly, "The Company welcomes you back from hell, Son."

"My name is Kadri Tabak. I am the Turkish OHD Chief Agent." He then embraced Alev, kissed her on both cheeks, and whispered something in her ear.

"I'm Ariel Mazar, Israeli Mossad." The attractive, middle-aged woman smiled and then nodded acknowledgements at Ari and Zivah.

"Cheerio! I am William Thomas, British MI6." Shaking Logan's hand, he stated, "If you were not already knighted, my dear chum, I would propose that the Queen promptly do so!"

Colonel Connery then declared, "Because you completed your dangerous mission with honor, the joint agencies are giving Commendations of Courage to each of you." Holding up a gold medal, he continued, "Perhaps more importantly, the CIA is pleased to present this Medal of Valor to Agent Ari Jacobi in recognition of being wounded in battle."

Ari protested, "But, it's merely a flesh wound."

The entire roomful of experienced espionage agents laughed at Ari's comment and clapped for him. Pat added, "You earned it, my friend. You really earned it!"

One by one, starting with Pat and ending with Zivah, the operatives related their mission stories in great detail. Officers from all four agencies interrupted occasionally to clarify fine points.

After several hours of debriefing, Connery said, "Let's break for lunch and meet back here at 1500 hours. That will give us time to convey our initial findings and recommendations to our agencies' headquarters. Make sure you take all of your notes and belongings with you."

As they left the conference room, Alev asked her comrades, "Shall we walk down Ataturk Boulevard a few blocks? There's a nice little restaurant there that I frequent, and they serve excellent grilled sea bass, and delicious lamb kabobs."

"Let's go for it!" Pat responded.

The five operatives enjoyed a fine meal enhanced with domestic Doluca wine. Then they started to leisurely stroll back to the Ankara Hilton. Just past the Ethnography Museum, they stopped to look at a brass shop's window display.

Pat noticed a reflection in the window of someone lingering suspiciously half a block behind them. He warned his team, in a low voice, "Don't look now, but someone may be following us. He has a light complexion, graying hair, and he's wearing a dark-colored Western business suit. Alev, there's a large group of German tourists walking this way. When they reach us, we'll start talking to them. As we mingle with the Germans, you slip into the shop during the ensuing confusion. Peek out the window as the rest of us head toward the hotel, and determine if he really is tailing us."

"Okay, Patrick. I'll also see if I can identify him. Watch for my text message." The others nodded their acknowledgement, and all five mission team members were now in a red alert state . . . ready for action with a combat mindset.

Hidden behind two huge bas-relief decorated brass trays in the window display, Alev waited for the subject to pass by. The man soon appeared, and he then stepped into the entry alcove of the brass shop and put a hand inside his suit coat. Believing he was about to pull out a weapon, Alev immediately drew her 9-millimeter Zigana pistol and presented it toward the door with a two-hand hold while taking a combat stance. However, the subject pulled out a cell phone, made a call, and did not enter the shop. Alev thought, *That's Sergey Ivanov. I've seen him go in and out of the Russian Consulate. I believe he's a SVR agent.*

The man peered around the alcove to watch the other four operatives as they walked up the boulevard toward the Hilton. As he stepped back onto the sidewalk to follow them, Alev re-holstered her pistol and sent Pat a text message, *"viper leader. subject tailing you is sergey ivanov. works at russian consulate and may be svr. copperhead."*

Pat responded, *"copperhead. just pursue for now. svr may realize we were involved in the demise of andrei desnov in tehran. take him out if he starts anything. viper leader."* He told his other operatives, "Alev has our backs. The subject may be a Russian agent, but she can handle him."

The Russian followed Pat, Ari, Logan, and Zivah to their hotel, and Alev followed the Russian. As the four operatives entered an elevator, Ivanov slipped into the lobby and took a seat in the reading area. He then feigned browsing through a newspaper while observing the elevator and front desk areas.

Alev entered the hotel right behind him and talked a bellhop into letting her use the service elevator so the Russian would not see her. She caught up with the others in front of the Ararat Conference Room, and told the agents guarding the door about Ivanov. Then the five operatives entered the room. Pat addressed the headquarters officers after closing the door, "A potential SVR agent, Sergey Ivanov from the Russian Consulate, tailed us from a restaurant down the boulevard. He's in the lobby and needs to be dealt with."

Tabak immediately made a call on his cell phone and spoke Turkish rapidly for a few minutes. Alev whispered to her comrades, "It's done. Ivanov will not be seen in Ankara again, or perhaps any other place."

The colonel then reconvened the meeting with, "The room has been swept for listening devices again, and it's clean, so we can speak freely. Now that the immediate problem with the Russian is resolved, we can begin. Based on what we've learned so far, our agencies have developed the following preliminary plans." He projected a map of Iran on a wall screen with his notebook computer's PowerPoint program. The map displayed Iran's known nuclear research and development sites.

Pointing at each site location on the map, from north to south, he continued, "Our top brass approved a conditional joint plan to destroy the nuclear facilities at Chalus, Tehran, Parchin, Qom, Arak, Isfahan, Natanz, Darkhovin, Ardakan, Bushehr, and Fasa. Although their nuclear infrastructure may include up to 300 sites, these actions will eliminate the Islamic Republic of Iran's capability to develop nuclear weapons for at least 10 years. During that time, there might be another revolution and a more reasonable government may then be running the nation."

"Our pre-emptive strikes may even trigger the overthrow of the current regime by opposition groups, like the Iranian People's Mujahedeen and the Jundallah of Iran," Logan offered.

Ari added, "And don't forget the Democratic Party of Iranian Kurdistan and other National Council of Resistance of Iran members."

"Also, Tondar, another anti-Islamic government faction," Zivah offered.

Pat asked the colonel, "When do we plan to hit them?"

"We'll take them out with conventional weaponry soon, on a day to be determined by the joint forces. All of the aforementioned nuclear facilities will be destroyed simultaneously by an international strike force from the U.S., Turkey, Israel, and the U.K.

"As you know, Iran's current president has constantly defied all U.N. resolutions regarding his nation's nuclear research and development. Just recently, their Atomic Energy Organization chief announced they will soon commission additional nuclear installations at undisclosed locations throughout the nation. Moreover, Intel believes they may have a nuclear warhead soon. Iran will also have an intercontinental ballistic missile that can reach the U.K. and perhaps the U.S. within a year, and they already have the largest ballistic missile inventory in the Middle East. Therefore, we must stop them in their tracks, right now!"

Zivah spoke up, "Can you give us the details of the strikes? I'm particularly interested in Israel's role."

"Yes, Agent Benjamin, I'll cover the strikes on each site in detail, starting in the north and ending in the south. Please observe the map. Fighter jets flying at high altitudes will launch Miniature Air-Launched Decoys at each of the nuclear sites. The MALDs will mimic combat aircraft and trick the anti-aircraft guided missile batteries guarding the primary targets into activating their radar systems. This will reveal their positions. The same fighter jets, still flying at high altitudes, will then conduct air strikes on the hidden anti-aircraft locations using AGM-65E2/L air-to-surface laser-guided missiles. These are 'fire and forget' ASMs equipped with shaped-charge, high-explosive warheads."
As the colonel highlighted each location on the map with a laser pointer, they appeared to radiate on the projection

screen with flashes of light simulating the destruction of the missile batteries. "Are there any questions at this point?" No one spoke up.

Connery continued, "The primary targets, which of course are the nuclear sites, will then be destroyed with 'shock and awe' pre-emptive air strikes by the fighter jets, and in some cases, by bombers protected by the fighter jets. The fighters will carry satellite-guided, synchronized 500-pound bunker-busting smart bombs to use on most of the targets. They can penetrate up to 14 feet of reinforced concrete. They will also utilize air-to-surface guided missiles on some of the softer targets.

"The bombers will carry satellite-guided 30,000-pound Massive Ordnance Penetrator bombs, which will be used on the Chalus, Qom, and Isfahan hardened underground sites. The MOP is a newly developed technology that is ten times more powerful than previous bunker-busters. Moreover, they can penetrate 200 feet of reinforced concrete and 130 feet of hard rock. MOPs are designed to explode 200 feet below ground level." He again highlighted each location on the map with his laser pointer and the nuclear sites appeared to explode into puffs of smoke on the projection screen. "Now, what questions do you have?"

Pat responded, "This is a well thought out plan."

Zivah chimed in, "Yes, it is . . . but, I still want to know what role my country will play."

"Patience. I'm coming to that. Finally, commando raids will be conducted on what is left of the three hardened underground nuclear research sites to ensure their total destruction."

Pointing at Zivah, Colonel Connery continued, "Agent Benjamin, now what you are patiently waiting for . . . the players. Kadri Tabak will cover the next segment of the plan. Tabak?"

"Turkish Air Force F-35 Lightning II fighter jets will take out the missile batteries at the Chalus Weapons Development Facility. They will also fly protective cover for a U.S. Air Force B-2 Stealth bomber while it drops two 30,000-pound MOPs on the hardened nuclear site. The fighters will escort the B-2 in and out of Iranian air space."

Alev added, "That site is so remote, we will not have to be concerned about innocent civilian causalities. However, it is really hardened deep into the tall mountain. It might take an earthquake to destroy it!"

Connery responded, "Who knows? Maybe the two MOPs *will* trigger an earthquake and finish the job for us." Addressing Pat, he said, "U.S. Air Force F-115E fighter jets will take out the missile batteries near the Tehran Nuclear Research Center and at the Parchin facility. The same jets will subsequently drop 500-pound bunker-buster bombs on these softer sites . . . which will include the Parchin nuclear explosion mock-up site, nuclear test tunnel, and the Chemical Weapons Factory."

Pat spoke up, "I'm not concerned with civilians near the remote Parchin site. However, I am worried about civilian casualties around the congested metropolitan Tehran site."

The colonel replied, "Agent O'Leary, our precision smart bombs and missiles will take out *only* the targets. Civilians on the street or in surrounding buildings will be safe from harm." Pointing at the map, he continued, "Another U.S. F-115E fighter group will take out the missile batteries guarding the Qom tunnel construction site. Similar to the raid at Chalus, the fighters will also fly protective cover for a U.S. B-2 while it drops two MOPs on the hardened future nuclear site. They will escort the B-2 in and out of Iranian air space."

Looking at Ari, Connery said, "Ariel Mazar will present the next segment. Mazar?"

"Agent Jacobi, Israeli Air Force F-161 Sufa fighter jets will take out the missile batteries at the Arak Heavy-water Reactor site. The same fighters will subsequently drop 500-pound bunker-buster bombs on that softer nuclear site."

"That's good. There aren't any civilians near the remote site," Ari said.

Colonel Connery nodded in acknowledgement. Pointing at Logan, he stated, "William Thomas is up next. Thomas?"

"Agent Johnson, U.K. Royal Air Force Eurofighter Typhoon FGR4 fighter jets will take out the missile batteries at the Natanz Uranium Enrichment site. They will subsequently drop 500-pound bunker-buster bombs on that softer nuclear site."

Logan interrupted, "Just as at Arak, Natanz is so isolated there will not be civilian causalities there."

"You are absolutely correct, my good man," Thomas responded.

Nodding and winking at Zivah, Colonel Connery said, "Now, back to Ariel Mazar."

"Agent Benjamin, another Israeli F-161 fighter group will take out the missile batteries protecting the Isfahan Administrative Offices and the Research Center. The F-161s will subsequently use air-to-surface laser-guided missiles to destroy the Administrative Offices. They will also drop 500-pound laser-guided bombs on most of the softer Research Center buildings. Similar to the raids at Chalus and Qom, the fighters will also fly protective cover for a U.S. B-2 while it drops two 30,000-pound MOPs on the hardened underground site at the Research Center. Those same fighters will escort the B-2 in and out of Iranian air space."

Zivah chimed in, "Civilians at the isolated research facility are not a problem. However, they are at the administrative offices in town. I've arranged for the university students to be away from the campus the day we take out that site. But, we need to get word to my contact as soon as you have a firm strike date."

The colonel responded, "Agent Benjamin, we've already advised Farah that we will give her the firm strike date. We will also notify our *Irani* mole in the administrative offices. Moreover, we appreciate *everyone's* concerns for innocent civilians."

Connery continued his part of the presentation, "Meanwhile, in the Persian Gulf area, two squadrons of U.S. Navy F/A-18F fighter jets will utilize air-to-surface laser-guided missiles and 500-pound laser-guided bombs to destroy the Darkhovin Uranium Enrichment Site and the Ardakan Uranium Ore Purification Plant."

Then Mazar added, "At the same time, two squadrons of Israeli F-161s will hit the Bushehr Light-water Nuclear Reactor and the Fasa Uranium Conversion Facility with the same weapons."

The colonel asked, "Now, what questions do you have?"

Ari spoke up. "Colonel, how about the commando raids you mentioned earlier?"

"That's the concluding part of our presentation, Agent Jacobi. Tabak . . . It's your's again."

"After the bomb strikes, Turkish *Maroon Beret* commandos transported by Eurocopter AS-532UL Cougar helicopters and escorted by Turkish F-35s will raid the hardened target at Chalus."

Connery continued, "American *Delta Force* commandos transported by CH-47F Chinook helicopters and escorted by U.S. F-115Es will attack the hardened target at Qom."

Mazar added, "A joint force of Israeli *Sayert Matkal* and British *Special Air Service* commandos will hit the hardened

Isfahan Research tunnel. The Israeli commandos will be transported by Sikorsky S-70 Blackhawk helicopters and escorted by Israeli F-161s." She pointed at William Thomas.

Thomas concluded her presentation, "The British commandos will be transported by Merlin HC3 helicopters and escorted by U.K. FGR4s."

The colonel added, "The joint forces will ensure the total destruction of all three of the hardened sites, and then immediately get the hell out of there."

"Wow!" Zivah exclaimed. "That should take care of Iran's nuclear weapon aspirations."

Not to be out done by Zivah, Alev remarked, "And more dirty camels will bite the dust!"

Colonel Connery concluded the presentation with, "Well, that's it. The debriefing will continue here tomorrow at 0800 hours. We'll give each of you SitReps after the fireworks. Remember; *do not* discuss these plans outside of this room."

While walking out of the conference room, Alev addressed her comrades, "I promised to show you the sights in Old Ankara. Shall we go?"

The other four mission operatives said, "Yes," enthusiastically.

Pat added, "We certainly made a great team, and this may be our last night together before we leave for our next assignments. So, let's relax and enjoy each other's company."

Alev made a call with her cell phone, and then said, "An OHD limo will be waiting for us in front of the hotel."

Zivah suggested, "Let's freshen up first." The others agreed.

They were heading across town a short while later. Like an experienced tour guide, Alev pointed out the city sights as they whizzed by. "That's the General Mustafa Kemal Ataturk monument high on the hill above us. The mausoleum has a commanding view of the capital city." The melodic call to evening prayer emitted from a loudspeaker in one of the minarets as they drove past a huge mosque. Alev continued, "This is the Yeni Mosque. It's the largest Ottoman era mosque in Ankara." Nearing their destination, she playfully asked, "Belly dancers first?" as she wiggled her torso provocatively.

Pat said, "Of course." The others nodded in agreement.

As the limo chauffeur drove up the hill toward Old Ankara, Alev declared, "On the right is my favorite place to pray to Allah . . . the Aslanhane Mosque."

After an enjoyable evening of sightseeing, exotic entertainment, and dining on delicious Turkish cuisine, the five operatives headed back toward the Ankara Hilton Hotel.

"Alev, I've enjoyed belly dancing shows in Morocco, Egypt, Greece, Jordan, Israel, Paris, New York, and San Francisco. However, the performance tonight was the best I have ever seen. Thank you for escorting us during our last hours together," Pat declared.

Alev giggled and replied coyly, "The two dancers you saw tonight are my cousins."

Zivah then commented, with a warm smile, "Alev, thank you for being our guide. This was a delightful excursion, and I saw another side of you that I thoroughly enjoy and respect."

"I too am pleased with your company, Zivah, and I believe we can now be good friends. After all, our two governments *did* establish close military relations in 1996," Alev replied pleasantly. Both female operatives laughed, and the tension between them immediately dissolved.

The amicable exchange prompted Logan to say, "It's about time you two got along!"

Pat said, "Ditto."

Ari just grinned.

Back at the Hilton Hotel, the operatives exited the limo and the driver went into the hotel for a cold drink.

On his balcony, under a romantic silvery moon, Pat confided in Zivah, "I just learned that I'm being sent to Tel Aviv to work with Mossad as the CIA's Chief Middle East Liaison Agent. Did you have anything to do with that?"

With a twinkle in her eyes, Zivah smiled sweetly and responded, "Who? Me?" Embracing Pat, she looked up at him and continued, "Patrick, Dear, we do get along well, and I love having you by my side at night. So, I did have a chat with Ariel Mazar, and you and I will be working together again. Besides, you know we both believe in the same Yahweh!"

"Sounds good to me, My Love! How about unwinding from the pressures of the mission first? We can spend a few days on the sunny beaches of Cyprus, Aphrodite's island, while en route to Israel."

"Excellent idea, Dear! Maybe we can find a golden sand beach in a secluded cove and go skinny-dipping in the warm Mediterranean, just as the Greek goddess of love and beauty did," Zivah gleefully replied as she pressed her firm breasts into Pat's chest.

As the two lovers kissed on the balcony, the OHD limousine parked below them in front of the hotel blew up. With his ears ringing, and nearly deafened from the concussion and loud sound of the blast, Pat pointed at a man with Iranian features standing under a street light a half a block away. He was smoking a cigarette while talking on a cell phone and grinning from ear-to-ear at the spectacle. Not able to hear himself talk, Pat shouted at Zivah, "I think he's a VEVAK agent!"

APPENDIX

Principal Characters

Location Code Names

Mission Timeline

Glossary

Afghanistan Map

Iran Map

Iraq Map

Turkey Map

Principal Characters

Patrick (Pat) O'Leary: American CIA agent and mission team leader, Code Name *Viper Leader*.

Hossein: Patrick's Iranian contact.

Alev Barak: Turkish OHD agent and mission team member, Code Name *Copperhead*.

Hamideh: Alev's Iranian contact.

Ari Jacobi: Israeli Mossad agent and mission team member, Code Name *Asp*.

Sadar: Ari's Kurdish contact.

Logan Johnson: British MI6 agent and mission team member, Code Name *Adder*.

Farhad: Logan's Iranian contact.

Zivah Benjamin: Israeli Mossad agent and mission team member, Code Name *Cobra*.

Farah: Zivah's Iranian contact.

Andrei Desnov: Russian SVR agent.

Doctor Ali Kermani: Iranian VEVAK agent.

Hassan Degani: Iranian VEVAK agent.

Sergey Ivanhov: Russian SVR agent.

Location Code Names

Alpha:	Istanbul
Bravo:	Van
Charlie:	Tabriz
Delta:	Tehran
Delta One:	Tehran Nuclear Research Center
Echo:	Parchin Nuclear Research and Chemical Weapons Facility
Foxtrot:	Chalus
Foxtrot One:	Chalus Nuclear Weapons Development Facility
Golf:	Hamadan
Hotel:	Arak Heavy-water Nuclear Reactor
India:	Ahvaz
Juliet:	Ardestan
Kilo:	Natanz Uranium Enrichment Center
Lima:	Isfahan
Lima One:	Isfahan Administration Offices
Lima Two:	Isfahan Nuclear Technology and Research Center
Mike:	Ankara

Mission Timeline

MISSION TIMELINE

OPERATIVE	DAY 1	DAY 2	DAY 3	DAY 4	DAY 5	DAY 6	DAY 7	DAY 8
PATRICK *Viper Leader*	Istanbul to Tabriz	Tabriz to Tehran	Tehran	Tehran to Parchin to Tehran	Tehran to desert	desert to Tabriz	Tabriz to Ankara	Ankara
ALI V *Copperhead*	Istanbul to Tabriz	Tabriz to Chalus	Chalus	Chalus to Tabriz	Tabriz	Tabriz	Tabriz to Ankara	Ankara
ARI *Asp*	Istanbul to Hamadan	Hamadan to Arak to Hamadan	Hamadan	Hamadan to Tabriz	Tabriz	Tabriz	Tabriz to Ankara	Ankara
LOGAN *Adder*	Istanbul to Ahvaz	Ahvaz to Ardestan	Ardestan to Natanz to Yazd	Yazd	Yazd to Zahedan	Zahedan to Kandahar	Kandahar to Ankara	Ankara
ZIVAH *Cobra*	Istanbul to Isfahan	Isfahan	Isfahan	Isfahan to Yazd	Yazd to Zahedan	Zahedan to Kandahar	Kandahar to Ankara	Ankara

Glossary

AEHF:	Advanced Extremely High Frequency satellite system
Aga:	Mister (Per.)
Allah o Akbar:	God is Great (Arab.)
ASAP:	As soon as possible
As salam'alakoom:	Greetings (Arab.)
Badgirs:	Wind funnel cooling towers (Per.)
Bakeesh:	Bribe (Per.)
Baklava:	Near East pastry (Turk./Greek)
Baleh:	Yes (Per.)
Beryani-Biryani:	Ground lamb dish cooked on one side (Per.)
Booroh:	Go (Per.)
Chador:	Full-length veil (Per.)
Chahee:	Tea (Per.)
Chelo kebab:	Rice and lamb kebab; Iran's national dish (Per.)
Chihil Sutun:	Forty Pillars (Per.)
CIA:	American Counter Intelligence Agency
Ciao:	So long; goodbye (Italian)
Da:	Yes (Russ.)

Daas vee daan ya!:	Goodbye! (Russ.)
Dasht:	Desert; wilderness (Per.)
Dhow:	Boat (Arabic)
Djellaba:	Desert robe (Arab.)
Dolmas:	Grape leaves stuffed with rice and meat (Turk./Greek)
Efendi:	Sir (Turk.)
Enshallah:	God willing; will of God (Per.)
Farsi:	Persian language (Per.)
Gharm:	Hot (Per.)
Ghosht-en-khor-est:	Stew (Per.)
Hale shoma chetowre?:	How are you? (Per.)
Hijab:	Islamic dress code for women (Arab.)
Humvee:	High-mobility Multipurpose Wheeled Vehicle
IAEA:	International Atomic Energy Agency
Imam:	Islamic priest; saint (Arab.; Per.)
Intel:	Intelligence
Irani:	Iranian (Per.)
Jangal:	Forest; jungle (Per.)
Jihad:	Holy War (Arab., Per.)
Jubes:	Deep gutters (Per.)

Kaku sabzi:	Caviar and egg frittata (Per.)
Kal:	Goodbye (Turk.)
Khanom:	Wife (Per.)
Kharahb:	Awful, terrible (Per.)
Keffiyah:	Desert headdress (Arab.)
KGB:	Russian Committee for State Security (now SVR)
Khoda Hafez:	Go with God (Per.)
Khoob, merci maemnum:	Good, thank you (Per.)
Kuche:	Side street; alley (Per.)
MALD:	Miniature Air-Launched Decoy
MAV:	Micro Aerial Vehicle
Merci:	Thank you (Fr., Per.)
MI6:	British Secret Intelligence Service
MOP:	Massive Ordinance Penetrator
Morg Polow:	Rice with Chicken (Per.)
Mossad:	Israeli Institute for Intelligence and Special Operations
Muezzin:	Islamic caller of the faithful to prayer (Per.)
Mullah:	Muslim educated in Islamic theology and sacred law (Per.)

Namez:	Islamic prayer five times a day (Per.)
Nan-e-bahr-bahr-ee:	Thick flat bread (Per.)
Nan-e-lavash:	Paper-thin unleavened flat bread (Per.)
Nan-e-tafttoon:	Round, soft, flat bread (Per.)
NATO:	North Atlantic Treaty Organization
Now-Ruz:	New Year (Per.)
OHD:	Turkish Special Warfare Department
Panz:	Five (Per.)
Pasadaran:	Iranian Revolutionary Guard Corps (Per.)
Qanat:	Underground aqueduct (Per.)
Rial:	Iranian currency (Per.)
Rud:	River (Per.)
Salaam!:	Hello! (Per.)
SAVAK:	Iranian Secret Police (now VEVAK)
Sayert Matkal:	Israeli General Staff Reconnaissance commandos (Heb.)
Selam!:	Hello! (Turk.)
Shalom!:	Hello!; Goodbye!; Peace!; Health! (Heb.)
Sheol:	Hades (Heb.)

Shin Bet:	Israeli Internal Intelligence Agency (Heb.)
Si-o-se Pol:	Thirty-three arcade Bridge (Per.)
SVR:	Russian Foreign Intelligence Service
Toman:	10 *rials* (Per.)
Tout de suite:	Immediately (Fr.)
VEVAK:	Iranian Secret Police
Wadi:	Dry river bed (Arab.)

Afghanistan map

Iran Map

Iraq Map

TVRKEY

SYRIA

IRAQ

HALABAJAH

IRAN

JORDAN

N

BAGHDAD

KEY   OPERATIVE

3   Ari
4   Logan
5   Zivah

KVWAIT

SAVDI ARABIA

PERSIAN
GULF

© 2010 Bill Burke

Turkey Map

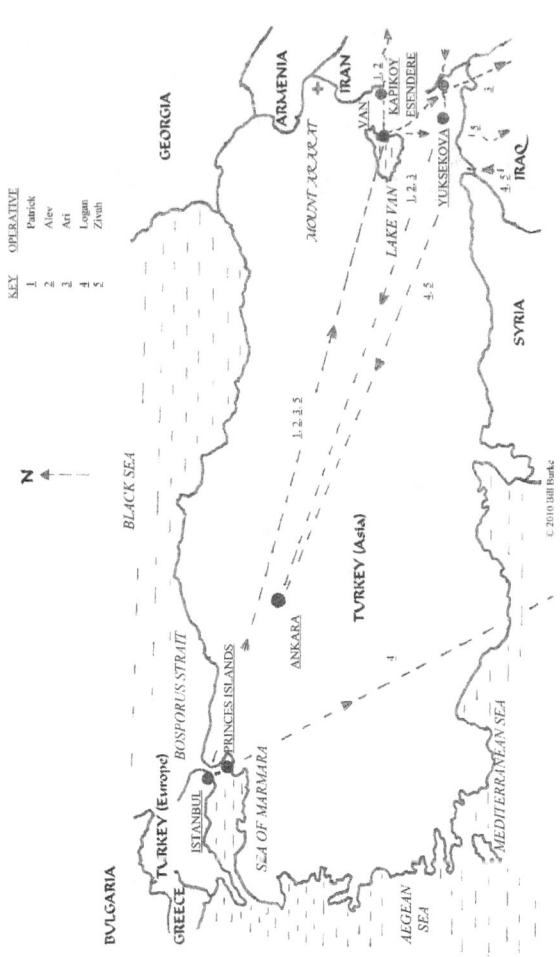

www.ingramcontent.com/pod-product-compliance
Lightning Source LLC
Chambersburg PA
CBHW071208260626
47162CB00004B/1225